She allowed **indulgence**

Awareness sizzled through her, followed by a shiver of caution. A man like him bore a warning label as clearly as if he'd had *Danger* embroidered across his butt in red silk floss. She hadn't noticed that he had turned to watch her over his shoulder, but now his grin was smug.

She had been wrong about one thing. Being strongly attracted to him wasn't the worst thing that could happen.

Having him know it was.

Dear Reader,

The Pacific Northwest, where I've spent most of my life, has been blessed with some of the most beautiful scenery on earth. One of my favorite places to explore is the Olympic Peninsula, with its craggy mountains and rocky beaches, rain forests and tidal pools. There are Victorian B and B's and lavender farms, Indian casinos and antique malls, aircraft carriers and car ferries. The coastline is bordered on three sides by an ocean, a foreign country and a crowded metropolis.

It's here that I've set the small town of Crescent Cove, filled with residents whose stories I hope to relate in this and future books.

Before I started writing, I was a dedicated reader of Harlequin Romance novels with two growing daughters and dreams of my own. The ways that people with their quirks and imperfections relate to each other, romantically and otherwise, have always fascinated me. When it comes to heroes, Prince Charming was never as compelling as the lion with the thorn in his paw, the beast who must learn to trust and to love.

My characters are not unlike the people we all know: our neighbors, family and friends. They have hopes and dreams and flaws, needs that must be met, problems that must be overcome and empty spots in their lives that must be filled. It is my pleasure and my passion to tell their stories in order to entertain my readers and, hopefully, to tug at their heartstrings.

Pam Toth

THE TENANT WHO CAME TO STAY

PAMELA TOTH

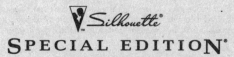

SPECIAL EDITION

Published by Silhouette Books

America's Publisher of Contemporary Romance

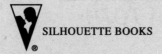 SILHOUETTE BOOKS

ISBN-13: 978-0-373-24768-4
ISBN-10:   0-373-24768-0

THE TENANT WHO CAME TO STAY

Visit Silhouette Books at www.eHarlequin.com

Printed in U.S.A.

Books by Pamela Toth

Silhouette Special Edition

Thunderstruck #411
Dark Angel #515
Old Enough To Know Better #624
Two Sets of Footprints #729
A Warming Trend #760
Walk Away, Joe #850
The Wedding Knot #905
Rocky Mountain Rancher #951
*Buchanan's Bride #1012
*Buchanan's Baby #1017
*Buchanan's Return #1096

The Paternity Test #1138
The Mail-Order Mix-Up #1197
*Buchanan's Pride #1239
The Baby Legacy #1299
Millionaire Takes a Bride #1353
†Cattleman's Honor #1502
†Man Behind the Badge #1514
†A Winchester Homecoming #1562
In the Enemy's Arms #1610
Prescription: Love #1669
The Tenant Who Came To Stay #1768

Silhouette Romance

Kissing Games #500
The Ladybug Lady #595

*Buckles & Broncos
†Winchester Brides

PAMELA TOTH

USA TODAY bestselling author Pamela Toth has written romance for over twenty years. She was born in Wisconsin but has spent most of her life near Seattle where she's raised two fantastic daughters, Erika and Melody, and a parade of Siamese cats.

Pam is married to her high school sweetheart, Frank. They live in a townhome with a view of Mount Rainier. When she's not writing, she enjoys traveling and antiquing with her husband, reading, quilting and doing counted cross-stitch. She's been a member of Romance Writers of America since 1982.

Fans may write her at P.O. Box 436, Woodinville, WA 98072 or visit her at www.specialauthors.com.

To Frank, my own romantic hero, who supports
and inspires me each day, and to everyone
who reaches out to the rest of us with tolerance,
acceptance, kindness and love.

Chapter One

Pauline Mayfield tossed and turned in her darkened room as the late spring storm howled outside her house. The Victorian structure had withstood similar storms for more than a century, she reminded herself silently, and it would stand up to this one, as well. As the rain battered her bedroom windowpane like pellets from a shotgun, she pulled the covers over her head and tried to sleep.

Suddenly there was a loud cracking sound from outside, followed by an explosive crash. Her eyes flew open and she sat bolt-upright, afraid to breathe, but all she could hear was the wind and the rain.

Heart thudding, she hurried to the window. Her breath fogged the glass, making it impossible to see into the night. Worried that a tree might have flattened her

SUV, she threw on her bathrobe. When she reached the hall, another door opened and an elderly woman poked her white head out from her bedroom.

"What was that horrible noise?" she demanded, her British accent more pronounced than usual. "For a moment I thought I was back in the blitz."

"It's okay, Dolly." Pauline barely paused to give her a reassuring smile. "I'll check outside."

"Take an umbrella so you don't get soaked," Dolly replied before she shut her door.

When Pauline reached the laundry room, she thrust her bare feet into a pair of rain boots. Muttering a quick prayer, she flipped on the outdoor light. From the back porch, she saw her undamaged SUV, but her relief was short-lived.

She grabbed the flashlight from its hook inside the door and clumped down the steps, clinging to the porch railing so the boots wouldn't trip her.

The strong wind blew open her robe, and the rain soaked the front of her thin nylon gown. The wet fabric pressed against her bare skin, chilling her as she belted her robe. Shivering, she fumbled with the latch on the backyard gate.

Her boots threatened to slip off her feet with each step she took, and the wind blew her wet hair into her eyes as she aimed her flashlight beam at the garage. A fallen limb from the towering cottonwood tree lay sprawled on the roof.

Pauline felt as though a ball of yarn had risen into her throat. Swallowing hard, she told herself that the damage to the former carriage house might not be as bad as it appeared.

Assessing the damage or tarping the roof before morning was more than she could manage. Meanwhile, she was getting soaked for nothing. Fighting back tears of frustration, she returned to the house, where she struggled with dripping hair and stubborn boots.

Dolly appeared in the kitchen doorway and handed Pauline a towel. "Could you see anything?" she asked.

Thanking her, Pauline wrapped the towel around her head. "A limb fell onto the garage roof," she said through clenched teeth. "I'll call Steve Lindstrom in the morning and see if he can check it out."

"You're soaked," Dolly exclaimed. "Go take a hot shower while I make you some tea."

Pauline doubted she could swallow anything, but she didn't want to be rude. "Good idea," she replied. "Thanks."

To Dolly, tea was a sure cure for just about anything. But Pauline just wanted to wake up and find out this was all a bad dream.

Early the next morning Pauline stood in her driveway and shielded her eyes against the May sunshine that seemed to mock her with its brightness. She watched as her contractor buddy, Steve Lindstrom, stepped down off the ladder he'd propped against her garage. He'd come right over when she'd phoned him even though he must have gotten a dozen other calls.

"I hope you're going to tell me the damage isn't as bad as I thought and that it won't cost me a big bag of money," she implored, exhausted from her sleepless night.

Steve picked up his clipboard and straightened, towering over her in his heavy boots. His solid build might have been intimating if she hadn't known him since high school, when he and her little sister had been a hot item.

Pauline had always been immune to the younger man's hunky charm. His sun-streaked hair—badly in need of a trim, as usual—poked out from under his red baseball cap. Beneath his thick mustache, his smile was sympathetic. "You know, I wouldn't be doing my job if I lowballed the cost," he replied. "Have you called your insurance agent?"

"He promised to stop by later, but he warned me a while ago that I was underinsured," she admitted.

"I don't suppose you listened," Steve guessed.

Pauline shook her head. "Worse than that, I jacked up the deductible to save a few bucks on the premium."

"By how much?" he asked.

When she told him, he whistled softly. "Oh, boy, that bites. But you know I'll do the best I can to be fair."

"I know you will," she told him as she led the way through the side garage door.

He looked around carefully, muttering to himself and making notes with a pencil stub, while she trailed after him. Perhaps the damage looked worse than it really was.

"What's the bad news?" she asked as soon as they got back outside.

He studied his clipboard with an unreadable expression. "Remove the limb and haul it away, repair the roof, fix the water damage to the inside, repaint…"

"I'll do the painting and whatever else I can," she said quickly. The last thing she needed right now was a huge bill eating up the money she had painstakingly scraped together.

He jotted down another note before sticking the pencil back into the pocket of his faded flannel shirt. "This is really rough, you understand. I'll have a better idea after I make some calls and run the numbers, but replacing those cedar shakes won't be cheap. You know they won't match the rest until they have a chance to weather. There are some composite shingles on the market that look authentic, if you want to put on a new roof instead."

He glanced toward the street. "No one would really notice, not with the garage sitting this far back."

"I'd notice," Pauline replied. "Just figure the cost of patching it, okay?"

"Sure thing." He scratched his chin and named a figure that unhinged her jaw and made it drop. "If I find more damage behind that soggy plasterboard, the cost will climb," he cautioned.

She groped for something positive to head off her mounting hysteria. "At least I can burn the wood." Heating oil was expensive, but the big old house was blessed with working fireplaces in nearly every room.

"Sorry, hon, but cottonwood burns too hot for an indoor fire," he replied. "It wouldn't be safe."

Muscles flexing in his arms and shoulders, he loaded the metal ladder onto the white truck that was parked in the long gravel driveway. Lindstrom Construction, it said on the door in plain black letters, followed by a local phone number.

Already the sun had dried up the puddles she'd stepped over earlier.

"Figures," she grumbled, fiddling with her chunky beaded bracelet. This setback was only temporary, but she wouldn't let it derail her plans.

He closed the tailgate and walked around to the cab. "I gotta tell you up front that I don't know when I can get to it."

When he opened the door of the truck, she noticed that the passenger seat was littered with papers. An empty coffee cup sat in the holder on the dash and a badly faded tassel from two years behind her own graduation dangled from the rearview mirror. "I'm slammed with work and I just lost my best guy to a builder in Bremerton," he added.

Anxiously Pauline scanned the horizon for signs of another storm moving in from the Strait. All she could see was an endless expanse of bright blue sky. But dark rain-swollen clouds could roll off the Olympics or blow down from Canada at any time, just as they had last night.

Steve must have noticed the direction of her gaze. "I'll send someone over to tarp the roof. Be sure to open the windows so the inside will dry out."

"I can't thank you enough," she said as he tossed the clipboard into the truck and got behind the wheel.

She wondered whether he ever thought of Lily now that he was divorced. He never asked Pauline about her—not that she would have much to tell him if he did.

"Either Brian or the new guy I hired will be over later," he said through his open window.

Brian was a gangly teenager who had mowed her

lawn every summer until he'd graduated from the local high school and begun working full-time for Steve.

He started the engine, then glanced around at the garage. "Don't you worry about the money." He flicked the point of his shirt collar with his finger. "Maybe you could monogram these for me in trade."

The idea of a monogram on the faded material made her smile. "I'd be happy to." She glanced at her watch. "I've got a class in half an hour, so I'd better get going. Thanks so much for coming."

"No problem." With a wave, he pulled out his cell phone as he went back down the driveway and turned onto the street.

Pauline thrust aside her concerns and hurried across the gravel to her SUV. The last thing she needed was a group of cranky old blue-hairs clustered on the sidewalk in front of her shop, bad-mouthing her for her lack of punctuality.

Wade Garrett had just driven straight up from San Francisco to Crescent Cove. Nearly swaying from fatigue, he was in no mood for jokes as he stared down at the short man with the bad comb-over who stood fidgeting in front of him.

Wade fixed Kenton Wallingford with a look he'd been told was intimidating enough to make an enemy spy rat out his own mother. "What did you just say to me?" Wade asked softly.

Wallingford took a step back as the toothpick in his mouth bobbed from one corner to the other. "I, uh, I said I can't rent you the cabin after all." The slack muscles in his wrinkled neck quivered visibly when he swallowed. "My sister showed up a couple of days ago with her two kids and a black eye," he whined. "What was I supposed to do, send her back to that bum I warned her not to marry ten years ago, so's he can knock her around some more?"

Frustrated, Wade rubbed his temple where a headache had begun keeping time with the throbbing bass pouring out of a car stereo idling out on the street. He felt like marching over and ripping it out with his bare hands.

"How long will they be here?" he asked with a longing glance at the cabin he'd leased over the Internet and where he'd planned on sleeping tonight. A kid's tricycle was parked in the driveway next to a pair of tiny sneakers.

Jeez, maybe he could rent a motel room for a few days.

"Until my sister gets on her feet or that no-good husband of hers sweet-talks her into going back to him." Wallingford lowered his voice. "Between you and me, I'm betting on the latter. Carol's too damned lazy to support herself."

His dry chuckle made Wade want to haul him up by his greasy collar and shake him. It was probably a good thing Wade didn't have the energy left for anything that strenuous.

"Good luck finding a room anywhere around here, what with the Arts Festival this weekend." Wallingford hitched up his sagging pants. "Busiest damn time of year, and I'm not collecting a dime in rent," he added morosely.

Wade couldn't scare up a lick of sympathy for the little toad's plight. All he wanted was to shower off the travel dust, fall into bed and sleep for fifteen hours. "Life isn't fair," he drawled.

Suddenly he remembered the folded paper in his shirt pocket and his mood brightened. "Well, I'm sorry about your sister," he said, fishing it out, "but you faxed me a signed copy of the lease. I sent back a deposit."

Wallingford's smile turned crafty. "Read the fine print," he replied around the toothpick as he jabbed a finger at the form. "Like I already said, it's a family emergency."

Wade skimmed the lease. When he reached the cancellation clause at the bottom, he swore under his breath.

It was uncharacteristic for him to ignore such important details, but he wasn't used to dealing with such an annihilating defeat as he'd recently experienced. All he had wanted when he'd left California was to put the ruins of everything for which he had worked so hard behind him. Apparently he was paying the price for his haste.

"Look, I'm not fussy." The desperation and the resignation he could hear in his own voice made him wince. "Can't you find me somewhere to bunk, at least for tonight?"

Maybe Wallingford had a couch that pulled out or a damned lounge cushion on his back porch that Wade could borrow. At six-two, he was too damned tall to sleep in his car.

"You can deduct it from what you owe me," he

added. Had Wallingford hoped Wade might forget about the healthy deposit he'd paid? Not a chance.

The other man spread his hands in a gesture of helpless regret. "I'd put you up in the spare room for nothing, I swear, but my daughter's home from Wazoo, over in Pullman." He cleared his throat nervously. "Concerning the refund of your deposit—"

"I know," Wade cut in, smothering a yawn. "Read the fine print. Now you read my fine print and hand it over."

As soon as Wallingford pulled out his wallet and handed over a stack of bills, Wade jammed them and the useless rental agreement back into his pocket. He stalked back to his car, wondering if he should buy a sleeping bag and camp on the beach.

He was about to open his car door when Wallingford called out to him. "There's a garage apartment behind one of those old Victorians on Cedar, a couple of blocks over. I didn't hear of it being rented out." He pointed in the direction of a stand of tall firs. "The house is blue with purple trim and a big weeping willow tree in the front yard. You can't miss it."

Wade felt a twinge of hope. "Have you got the address?"

By the time Pauline had closed up her needlework shop on Harbor Avenue and driven back up the bluff to her house, her earlier anxiety had turned to dull resignation. She had no choice but to have the damage repaired as soon as Steve was available, no matter what the ultimate hit on her precious nest egg.

Mayfield Manor had been in her family for three

generations before she and her younger sister had in-
herited it. Even though Lily had obviously abandoned
the family home as well as her only living relative,
Pauline felt a deep obligation to maintain it. In addition
to her strong affection for the old house, she still clung
to her dream of someday replacing her female boarders
with a family of her own.

When she came around the corner of her street, she
saw the bright-blue tarp covering the corner of the
garage roof. Except for some sawdust and a few drag
marks in the gravel of her driveway, all signs of the
fallen limb were gone.

As soon as she emerged from her Honda with her
purse and her laptop, a dusty black car with out-of-state
plates pulled into the driveway behind her. Her elderly
boarder, Dolly Langley, was perched in the passenger
seat next to an unfamiliar man wearing sunglasses.

As Pauline waited, he got out from behind the wheel,
moving with surprising stiffness for someone with such
an athletic build. Nodding to Pauline, he circled the car
and opened Dolly's door. As spry as a little white-
headed bird, she hopped out, holding on to his hand.

"Pauline, wait till I tell you what happened," she
chirped in the British accent that all her years on this
side of the pond had failed to eradicate. "I found this
nice young man on my way home from the market."

Her satisfied smile stopped Pauline cold. Widowed
a decade before, Dolly insisted that a woman of Pauline's age could be neither happy nor complete without
a man to share her life. Had Dolly brought him home
for *her*, in the same way a cat might offer a dead mouse?

"I appreciate the endorsement," the stranger said in a husky voice as he bowed over Dolly's hand, "especially from a lady as lovely as you."

Dolly's wrinkled cheeks turned a delicate shade of pink, and she patted her tightly permed hair with her free hand while Pauline studied him with mixed wariness and curiosity. His black hair was cut short above his lean face. Even dressed as he was in a blue chambray shirt and jeans, stubble darkening his angular jaw, he would certainly be called a prize catch by most women.

Still clinging to his hand, Dolly tugged him forward, her eyes twinkling behind her trifocals. "Come and meet my landlady. She's the one I told you about."

Oh, Lord. Pauline's mind reeled at the possibilities her chatty boarder could have disclosed.

Maintaining an air of quiet dignity might have been easier if Pauline's blouse hadn't been streaked with dust from digging through freight, if her makeup hadn't completely worn off and her hair hadn't been restyled by the breeze blowing through her open car windows on her drive home.

As the man slipped off his sunglasses and tucked them into his pocket, she met his gaze squarely. Without the tinted lenses, his eyes were a startling shade of silver that contrasted sharply with his dark lashes. The intensity of his expression sent a shiver of awareness through Pauline as unwelcome as it was startling.

"This is Wade Garrett, fresh from San Francisco," Dolly said, releasing his hand. "Wade, Pauline Mayfield, my landlady."

Despite the polite smile that transformed his expression from intimidating to innocuous, Pauline hesitated before offering her hand.

She was being silly. As a member of the Waterfront Business Association and a candidate for the Crescent Cove city council, she had learned to cloak her shyness. Even so, his firm grip sent a jolt of reaction up her arm. Before she could identify the sensation, he released her.

"It's nice to meet you," he said with no indication that he, too, had felt the momentary shock.

"You, too," she replied automatically, relieved that she could speak without stammering. "And it was kind of you to give Dolly a ride."

"I was walking back from the market, and the strap on my grocery bag broke," Dolly interjected as he reached into his car, a luxury model beneath the road dust. "The oranges rolled right into the street, but he pulled over and chased every one of them down for me."

He held out the damaged bag to Pauline, who managed to take it without touching him again.

Dolly patted his bronzed forearm. "Where are you staying?" she asked him. "I'll bake you some nice banana bread. You aren't allergic to nuts, are you?" She glanced at Pauline. "I wouldn't want to be responsible for putting such a helpful person in the hospital."

"You don't have to do that," he protested, hooking one thumb into his wide leather belt. "I was actually on my way here when I stopped."

"Here to this house?" Dolly asked. "Well, isn't that nice."

He must have spread the tarp earlier, Pauline realized, wondering how he'd transported a ladder. Perhaps he had a truck, too.

"Let me show you the apartment above the garage," she said, reaching into her purse for her keys. "I keep the door locked."

His thick brows shot upward. "Did Wallingford call you already?" he asked. "That was quick."

Perplexed, Pauline hesitated. "*Kenton* Wallingford?" If Wade was connected with that no-good scam artist, she wasn't sure she wanted to have anything to do with him.

Wallingford had a reputation for get-rich-quick schemes that inevitably failed, taking other people's money in the process. "I don't know how you heard about me," she added, "but if you think the two of you can go around undercutting Steve Lindstrom's prices, you're sadly mistaken."

Wade held up his hands, palms outward as though to ward off a blow. "Whoa, hold on," he exclaimed. "I don't know about any damage and I have no idea who Steve might be—unless he's trying to rent the apartment from you, too."

"*Rent* it!" she echoed, shaking her head in confusion. "Why would Steve want to rent from me when he's got a perfectly nice house of his own? If you aren't here to repair the damages to my garage, why *are* you here?"

Dolly's bemused gaze shifted back and forth between them as though she were watching a tennis match on the telly, as she called it.

Wade narrowed his gaze. "My only connection to

that slimy scum-sucking weasel, Wallingford, is that after he took my deposit money and then broke the lease I had with him, he said you might have a vacancy over your garage."

"What a wonderful idea," Dolly exclaimed, clapping her hands. "That apartment has just been sitting empty."

"I'll take it," he replied, smoothing his hand over his close-cropped hair. "It's been a long day and I'm so dam—darned tired that I'm about to pass out."

"You poor man," Dolly exclaimed with an imploring glance at Pauline. "We just have to let him stay."

His fatigue was obvious and his situation unfortunate, but Pauline had no choice but to turn him down.

"A tree limb fell on the garage roof during the storm last night," she explained. "The apartment has a lot of water damage from the rain, especially the bathroom."

"How long will the repairs take?" he persisted.

The intensity of his gaze sent a shiver of reaction through Pauline, like some low-level jolt of electricity. Ever since he had first climbed out of his car, she had been trying to ignore the tug of attraction. If Dolly sensed it, she would hound them both.

"Steve hasn't given me a schedule yet." Pauline wished Wade would give up and go away so she could breathe normally.

"Ah, him again." Wade included Dolly in his half-hearted grin. "Wallingford warned me that every motel in town would be full because of some festival this weekend. Any suggestions of somewhere I could find a bed for tonight?"

None Pauline was about to voice out loud.

"Why don't you rent him a room in the house?" Dolly suggested. "The master suite is empty."

"I'll take anything," Wade said quickly. "And I'll be happy to provide references if you'd like."

"Oh, that's not necessary," Dolly replied breezily. "We know you're trustworthy."

And we know that how? Pauline wondered. Just because he'd picked up a few oranges and hadn't kept one for himself? "I don't think—" she protested.

"And you should give him a discount for that awful bedroom wallpaper," Dolly added firmly. "It's enough to give a monk nightmares."

Pauline *liked* the old-fashioned floral print, and Mr. Garrett didn't look like any monk she'd ever seen, but Dolly was on a roll.

"The suite does have a private bathroom with a claw-foot tub," she told Wade, "and a nice little sitting area that gets the morning sun. There's even a lovely desk and a matching chair, should you need a place to work."

"Sounds perfect." He looked at Pauline expectantly. "I'll risk the wallpaper. How much would you like up front?"

"I can't rent you the room," Pauline said firmly. "I'm sorry, but I don't take male boarders."

"You're kidding!" His smile disappeared abruptly. Without it, his thoughts were hard to guess, hidden behind his laser-sharp gaze. What if he was a lawyer contemplating a sexual discrimination case against her?

"Oh, Pauline, surely we owe him something," Dolly chided in her best retired-teacher's tone. "You could bend the rules this once."

* * *

"Rules?" Wade echoed as suspicions began to form in his overtired brain.

Wow, he had to hand it to old Mrs. Langley, who had fooled him completely. Despite her glasses, she must have the vision of an eagle to have spotted his California plates and dropped her grocery bag before he'd driven past her. Who would have thought the narrow, bumpy side street along the top of the bluff would be such a fertile hunting ground for desperate tourists in search of lodgings and con artists in search of victims?

Her granddaughter, on the other hand, wasn't nearly as good an actress. Her intentions were obvious—to express initial reluctance in order to wring as much rent money from him as possible.

He was about to ask whether Wallingford was also in on their scheme when a huge yawn overtook him. He swayed on his feet. By the time he'd managed to clamp his jaw shut, he realized that he didn't care what the room cost or how ugly its wallpaper was. If he didn't get horizontal soon, he'd fall asleep where he stood.

"But you'll make an exception for me, right?" He took out his wallet. "How much?"

Was that annoyance pleating her brow as she pushed her dark-blond hair off her forehead? Had he given in too quickly and ruined their little game?

"I'm sorry, but it wouldn't be fair to my other boarders," she insisted, spreading her hands wide like a supplicant pleading for understanding. "They don't expect to run into a half-dressed male in the upstairs hallway on their way down to breakfast."

"Which boarders might that be?" Dolly demanded, pushing her glasses up the bridge of her nose. "Not that tarted-up divorcée who'll be renting the Rose Room. And not me. That only leaves you to be affected by half-naked men, my dear." She parked her balled fists on her skinny hips. "Get over it."

Despite his exhaustion, Wade was amused—and rather touched—that she would champion him. Perhaps he had misinterpreted the situation entirely.

"What if I promise to keep my clothes on when I'm not in my room?" he asked, only half joking.

"It's not that," Pauline replied, ignoring his attempt at humor. "This is a small town."

He gaped at her. "And how is that a problem?"

"You probably won't understand." Her fair complexion had turned rosy with color. "It just so happens that I'm running for city council, and the locals tend to be pretty conservative—except for the shed people, of course, and the summer crowd that does whatever it wants and then leaves again."

Shed people? He was beginning to feel as though he had crossed more than a state border when he'd traversed the bridge over the Columbia River from Portland. Perhaps he had also wandered into some weird parallel universe.

"Fiddlesticks, it's not like the two of you will be staying alone in the house. I'll chaperone you," Mrs. Langley offered.

"There you go, Miss Pauline." Wade struggled to keep from shaking his head in disbelief. "Your good name will remain intact. Just tell me how much."

"It's not the money," she said.

As Wade groped for a way to change her mind, his glance swept past her SUV—an older model—to the house with its steeply pitched roof and ornate detailing. The light-blue exterior and purple trim were faded. The gravel driveway, although neatly edged and free of weeds, was rutted and uneven. Even the leaded windows in the double garage doors had two cracked panes.

It struck him that a place like this must need constant attention.

Without warning, Mrs. Langley reached up abruptly and squeezed his upper arm with her cold, bony fingers.

Struggling to smother yet another yawn, Wade nearly bit the tip off his tongue as his jaws snapped shut.

"What the hell are you doing?" he yelped, jerking away from her clutches.

"He's got some muscle there," she observed. "Perhaps we could put him to work."

Pauline was already shaking her head. "Never mind, Dolly. It's not a good idea."

"Balderdash!" Mrs. Langley exclaimed. "If you're worried, lock your bedroom door." She gave Wade a warm smile. "I can never remember to lock mine."

Good God, was the old gal *flirting* with him? As he stifled a chuckle, he realized where she was headed.

"What if I were to do the repairs to your garage," he asked, earning himself a wide grin from his elderly champion. "And I'll move out there as soon as possible." He'd worry about what he was actually getting into after he closed the deal.

Pauline's pretty hazel eyes widened. "Do you have remodeling experience?"

"Absolutely," he replied, his knotted muscles starting to loosen as he sensed her imminent capitulation. "I restored my first house in San Francisco." No need to add that he'd contracted out the plumbing and electrical work. What he didn't know, he'd find out.

Pauline threw up her hands in obvious resignation. "All right, you've got a deal. Maybe no one will notice that you're here."

Chapter Two

Pauline led her very first male boarder up the curved staircase to the second floor of her house, his solid tread thudding on the steps behind her as he toted his luggage. She could practically feel his gaze on her back, right between her shoulder blades.

If not lower.

Silently she reminded herself that she was a worldly woman of thirty-four, not an impressionable teenager. Even so, she couldn't remember the last time she had been so aware of a man's presence.

"That's a beautiful window," Wade said, glancing up when they reached the landing. "Is it original?"

"As far as I know." Pauline gazed fondly at one of her favorite features in the house, a round stained-glass image of a peacock. The jewel tones of the bird's intricately worked tail feathers glowed softly in the dying light from the sun.

Even though he had insisted that it wasn't necessary, pride wouldn't allow her to give him rooms that weren't spotless. She had whirled through the master suite with a vacuum cleaner and a dust cloth while Dolly had fed him a bowl of stew.

"You'll be here at the end," she said over her shoulder as they walked down the carpeted hallway. "There's a private sitting area as well as the bathroom Dolly mentioned."

"Have you owned the house for very long?" he asked.

Everyone in town knew Pauline's history. "I'm the fourth generation to live here," she explained, pausing. "My great-grandfather renamed it Mayfield Manor."

"It must be satisfying to have such a legacy," he remarked.

"I suppose. But growing up in a small town also has its disadvantages." She opened the double doors and stepped aside.

"Didn't get away with much, huh?" he teased with a wink as he walked past her.

"You could say that," she murmured, following him inside.

While she brushed a fleck of dust from the top of the tall dresser, he dropped his bags on the faded Persian rug next to the wide bed. Even though the burgundy draperies were open, she switched on the hanging teardrop lamp so the light shining through the blown-glass globe would add a rosy glow to the room.

"Wow," he said as he looked around. "I didn't expect anything like this."

Pauline wasn't entirely sure that his comment was positive. This had been her parents' private sanctuary, and she liked the traditional way her mother had redecorated it in shades of burgundy, dark green and cream. The bold floral wallpaper was a dramatic backdrop for the mahogany furniture and cream satin comforter.

Perhaps Wade preferred more modern decor, but this was an old house. With the exception of a few upgrades, it wore its age like a dowager who was well past her prime.

Feeling like an innkeeper, Pauline removed a folding suitcase stand from the tall wardrobe and set it next to the wood-burning fireplace. Faced in Minton tile, the hearth was bare for the summer behind the brass screen.

"Bathroom's in there," she indicated. "I hope you'll be comfortable here."

If he expected maid service, too, he was headed for disappointment. This wasn't a full-service rooming house, and she had neither the time nor the interest in pampering him.

"Right now the carpet would probably seem comfortable," he muttered, smothering a yawn.

"I'll bring you up some towels so you can get settled," she said. She'd forgotten them earlier.

His somber gaze softened into a smile, silver eyes crinkling slightly at the corners. His beard shadow gave him a rakish appearance. "Thanks again," he said, dismissing her. "Perhaps we can talk more in the morning."

Pauline was already having major second thoughts

about the situation, but it was too late now. She slid her hand into the pocket of her pants, her fingers touching the generous check he'd given her. The moment she had given in to her greed, he'd scrawled a rental agreement on the back of Wallingford's worthless lease. Dolly, ever helpful, had offered to witness his and Pauline's signatures.

"I leave for work at nine," she warned, 'aware of how small the bedroom seemed with both of them standing in it.

"I'm sure I can manage to be up by then." His grin displayed his even white teeth. If he had flaws, poor dental hygiene didn't appear to be one of them.

"Fine." She was irritated to realize she had been staring for a millisecond too long—and that his smile had widened just enough for her to be sure he had noticed.

Heat scorched her cheeks. "I'll get those towels."

It had been several years since Wade had experienced the momentary disorientation from waking up in unfamiliar surroundings. The big difference this morning was that he was alone in the bed.

He lay motionless, staring at the god-awful wallpaper with its blobs of color that reminded him all too clearly of a food fight back in his college frat house. Reality hit him with all the subtlety of the bright sunlight pouring through the drapes he'd forgotten to close before falling face-forward into bed. The last few months hadn't been a bad dream after all.

He was tempted to squeeze his eyes shut and pretend

that he was back in his elegant condo, French doors open to the breeze from the bay and his wife cuddled up beside him.

Ex-wife, he reminded himself, and good riddance to her. It was pointless to hang on to the fantasy of what his life had been; time instead to face the reality of what it had become.

He sat up with a groan, squinting at the mirror-topped dresser on the other wall. "Toto, we're not in San Francisco anymore," he muttered wryly, rubbing a hand over his face. Automatically he reached for the expensive watch Sharon had given him, but then he remembered that he'd sold it to a friend for half its value.

Flipping back the covers, he noticed an inexpensive clock radio next to a brass lamp with a fringed shade. If he was going to get downstairs before his landlady's departure, he'd better get his butt in gear.

He grabbed the shaving kit from his bag, stepped over his dirty clothes and stalked naked into the bathroom. Skidding to a stop, he stared at the old claw-foot monstrosity with disappointment. Tub baths were for kids and dogs.

As he tossed his kit onto the sink counter, he noticed a roomy shower stall behind a glass-block wall.

Hallelujah.

After he allowed the spray head to pummel him awake, he showered and shaved in record time. When he was done, he dug old jeans and a CBGB T-shirt from his bag and shook out the wrinkles.

Moments later he locked the door behind him as a clock from somewhere below chimed the quarter hour.

Before he reached the landing, another door opened and out stepped Pauline, wearing a blue dress with a rounded neckline and matching sandals that showed off her long legs. Some kind of clip held back the top of her honey-blond hair, but the rest hung loose, barely brushing her shoulders. She carried a laptop and a purse.

It occurred to Wade that he had no idea whether she worked as an attorney or a stripper. Even though he suspected that she had the body for the latter hidden beneath her outfit, the cut was too conservative and she was way too uptight.

Like a neglected house or an outdated stock portfolio, she had potential, which always intrigued him. The day was looking brighter.

"Good morning," he called out cheerfully. "It seems that I'm right on time."

When she turned, the tiny gold hoops in her ears winked in the light. "Did you sleep well?" she asked with a smile that softened her stern expression and stubborn chin. The transformation made him blink.

She had worked some female magic to play up her full lips and thick lashes. The scent of wildflowers— or what he imagined wildflowers would smell like— ensnared him.

"Like I'd been shot in the head," he replied.

"That's an image I'll try to forget." She gave an exaggerated shudder. "After all that rest, you're probably ready to get started on my roof."

"I'm rarin' to go," he drawled, realizing that he was famished. He would have to buy breakfast somewhere and then find a grocery store. Assuming he had kitchen privileges, he knew enough about cooking to keep himself fed.

"We can talk over breakfast, which Dolly usually fixes because she likes to cook," Pauline explained over her shoulder. "Lunch is on your own and dinner is potluck, depending on who's here and feels like fixing something. Or you can eat on your own, of course, if you'd rather."

"Sounds fine to me," he replied. "I'll be happy to kick in for groceries or go to the store. Just let me know."

"Don't worry, I will," she assured him.

At the bottom of the stairs, she led the way through the archway into the dining room he'd seen last night. A chandelier hung from the high ceiling above a dark wood table surrounded by matching chairs.

He followed her into the kitchen, which, like his bathroom, had obviously been modernized at some point, although the black-and-white-tiled floor looked original. The aromas of coffee and frying bacon made him realize how little he'd eaten in the last couple of days.

His attention went straight to Mrs. Langley, standing at the stove in a flowered apron over her purple sweat suit. On her feet were athletic shoes with fluorescent stripes, but he didn't care if she wore snowshoes as long as she fed him.

Mouth watering, he echoed Pauline's greeting.

"Good morning, you two," their cook responded gaily. "I hope you're hungry, because I'm making sourdough pancakes."

"Mrs. Langley, you've found my weakness," Wade replied, patting his empty stomach for emphasis. "I may just have to marry you."

With a girlish giggle, she waved him away with her spatula. "In that case, you'd better start calling me Dolly."

She opened the oven door, and Wade had to swallow hard in order to keep from drooling like a dog. "I'll set the table if you tell me where things are," he offered. Anything to hurry the process!

"In that drawer and the cupboard above it." Pauline pointed, then grabbed oven mitts. While he arranged the dishes and silver, she and Dolly brought over the food. He held out Dolly's chair as Pauline seated herself.

"If you wait, you lose," Dolly warned him as she reached for the coffeepot. "Help yourself."

They passed the food and filled their plates, though Pauline skipped the bacon and only took one pancake. It was all Wade could do to not grab everything in sight and cram it into his mouth.

"I must say, you look better than you did last night," Dolly told him as she stirred sugar into her coffee.

"I feel like a new man," he replied after he had swallowed his first bite of the best pancakes he'd ever tasted. A few trendy restaurants in Frisco would have killed for the recipe.

"These are fantastic," he added, reloading his fork.

"It's the starter," Pauline replied as she cut her pancake into neat, even pieces. "It was passed down from my grandmother."

"The what?" he asked blankly. Surely food that old couldn't be good.

"It's a mixture of flour, water and yeast," Dolly explained. "You keep adding to it so that it never runs out."

"I never knew that." He attempted to appear captivated, but Pauline distracted him.

In the light from the tall window, her hair was a mixture of shades from palest gold to rich, dark honey. He could almost feel it sifting through his fingers like warm silk.

"Something wrong?" she asked with a frown.

Feeling foolish for getting caught staring, he focused on his coffee. "I'm just enjoying the food and company."

"Will you be able to start on the repairs today?" she pressed.

He hoped she wasn't the type to stay on his back until the job was done, questioning every break he took and every penny he spent. "Absolutely," he replied.

When he saw the relief on her face, he felt a twinge of remorse. She had every right to be concerned about her roof. He remembered from vacation visits to his grandfather that this area was no stranger to summer rain.

"A buddy of mine is bringing my stuff up in a rented truck this afternoon," he added. "When I put it into storage, I'll unpack my tools. I'll write up a supply list after I buy groceries this morning."

Pauline actually grinned at him before glancing at her watch. "I'd better get going," she said, pushing back her chair. "Thanks for breakfast, Dolly."

"Do you have an account somewhere?" Wade asked as he got to his feet. Seeing Pauline's puzzled expression, he added, "So I can buy materials."

She nibbled on her full lower lip, sending a jolt of awareness through him. "I guess I could call the manager of the building-supply store and set it up," she murmured while he speculated on the softness of her mouth. "Greg and I went to school together, so it shouldn't be a problem."

"I'd better meet you there," he suggested quickly. "When we're through, I'll buy you lunch." Getting to know her better would be no hardship.

From behind her back, Dolly gave him a thumbs-up.

Pauline fiddled with a tendril of her hair. "Thank you, but that's not necessary." Her tone couldn't have been any prissier if he'd suggested a make-out session in the building supply parking lot.

Instinct warned him to proceed with caution. "I was just trying to avoid any delays," he said innocently. "But I can probably manage on my own."

Pauline carried her dishes through the arch to the kitchen and deposited them on the counter. "I'll give you my cell number," she said as Wade did the same. "You can let me know when you've got the list together." She opened her purse and handed him a card.

Uncommon Threads was printed in purple script. *Needlework supplies and classes, Pauline Mayfield, proprietor.* In smaller print was an address on Harbor Avenue, followed by phone and fax numbers. On the last line was an e-mail address.

He was impressed. "I'll look forward to seeing your shop," he said, tucking Pauline's card into his pocket.

Pauline finished her coffee at the sink, frowning at

him over the rim of her mug. "Are you sure you know what you're doing with my roof?"

"I worked summers as a carpenter when I was in college," he replied confidently.

"Any questions before I leave?" she asked as she put her mug into the dishwasher. "I've got to finish getting ready for work."

"If anything comes up," he replied, "we can discuss it at lunch."

She turned away without bothering to reply. A moment later he heard her footsteps on the stairs.

"Don't mind Pauline," Dolly told him as the two of them began cleaning up the kitchen. "Besides the repairs to the garage and managing her business, she's hoping to fill a vacated position on the city council."

"She's got a lot of irons in the fire," Wade replied thoughtfully as he loaded the dishwasher. "Breakfast was terrific. Since you cooked, I'll clean up the kitchen."

Dolly glanced at the clock on the front of the stove. "You'll do no such thing. I've got time before my soaps start, so you just go about your business and leave the kitchen to me."

"Okay, thanks." Wade drained the last of his coffee. "Could you point me in the direction of the nearest grocery store?"

After parking her SUV in its usual spot in a private lot behind one of Crescent Cove's old hotels, Pauline deposited Wade's rent check in the bank on the corner and then continued down the street to her shop.

Uncommon Threads was tucked into the heart of

the historic business district, which ran for several blocks along the waterfront. At one end was the ferry terminal. At the other, a small park with benches and a fishing dock that jutted into the bay.

Even though Pauline had probably walked down Harbor Avenue thousands of times, the flavor of the bygone era never failed to draw her attention. She glanced up at the tall buildings with their elaborate architecture and blank upper-story windows. Today they failed to distract her, as did the colorful hanging planters suspended from the old-fashioned streetlights.

Absently she waved at the city worker who watered the baskets and window boxes each morning, and at the meter cop who cruised by on her scooter. When the shops opened in less than an hour, the parking spaces along both sides of the street would all be taken. During the Arts Festival this weekend, the sidewalks and streets would be jammed with tourists from Seattle and beyond, who came to visit the galleries, buy souvenirs and tour some of the restored Victorian homes along the top of the bluff.

Pauline probably shouldn't even consider meeting Wade when she had so much stock to unpack and put out, but getting him started on the roof before another storm front blew through was important, too.

She paused in front of Uncommon Threads to admire the display of colorful pillows in the front window. Each one had been embroidered by a member of the local needlework guild using supplies from the shop. Because there was always room for improvement, she studied the grouping with a critical eye while she dug her keys from her shoulder bag.

When she opened the door, the scent of peach pot-pourri welcomed her into the shop's cozy interior. An old-fashioned glass display case and a service counter ran along one wall of the deep, narrow space that she had brightened with sunny yellow paint. On the other wall were shelves and pigeonholes full of fabric samples and threads from all over the globe. A row of circular display racks holding pattern charts and kits filled the middle of the main floor. Every bit of wall space was covered with a variety of finished projects: cross-stitched pictures, bell pulls, afghans, bookmarks and everything else that could be decorated with threads. Stairs led up to an overhead half loft she used for classes and extra storage.

The solid wood floor and the high ceiling were original. The water pipes in back rattled like chains on Halloween. The furnace was cantankerous. Summer business was crazy, winter nearly dead, ordering the right stock a crapshoot and staying in the black an ongoing challenge. Despite everything, Pauline dreamed of expanding.

After she put her purse and laptop in the tiny office tucked behind the staircase, she called Bertie Hemple-mann, an older woman who worked part-time in exchange for floss and fabric. Bertie agreed to fill in for a couple of hours so Pauline could leave.

With that problem solved, she counted money into the register and finished unpacking a carton of British cross-stitch books. While she worked, she hummed a jingle that had lodged into her brain on the way to work.

For the last five years, Uncommon Threads had been

hers. She loved every square inch of space and each moment she spent here. With each sale she made and each month she turned a profit, she took another small step toward regaining her self-respect and putting the past further behind.

At ten o'clock sharp she unlocked the front door and flipped the hanging sign from Closed to Open. When she wasn't helping the customers who trickled in, she unpacked cartons of kits, restocked the swivel racks and opened her morning mail. Along with a stack of invoices and bills was a brochure from a big needle-work show in the Midwest that made her salivate. Someday, she promised herself as the bell over the door jangled merrily, signaling a new arrival.

"Hi, Paulie," called out the tiny woman who owned the import shop next door. Lang, whose name meant "sweet potato" in Vietnamese, had elbowed open the door while she'd balanced a cardboard holder with two steaming lattes.

"Is it that time already?" Pauline asked, startled. She and Lang had gotten into the habit of sharing their morning break while Lang's husband, Dao, minded their shop next door.

Pauline bit her lip. "I'm going to be gone later, so I shouldn't take a break," she said after she'd thanked Lang for the hot drink.

"You want me to leave now?" Lang asked. "You need Howie to mind the store for you?" Howie was her American-born son who helped out in the family business part-time when he wasn't in school.

"No, stay," Pauline replied, blowing on her coffee to cool it. "It's okay. I called Bertie."

"You aren't unwell, are you?" Lang asked, perching on the spare chair behind the counter. It seemed as though the only times she or her husband ever missed work were to see the doctor or, once in a while, to watch Howie play baseball for the local high school team, the Bobcats.

Pauline was tempted to say she was going to see the insurance agent, since Lang knew about the damage to her garage roof. Instead she explained as briefly as she could about her new boarder.

Lang tipped her head to the side like a bird, her black eyes twinkling with mischief. "And this Mr. Wade, is he handsome?" she teased.

The heat that warmed Pauline's cheeks had nothing to do with the steam from her latte. "Um, I suppose." Her attempted nonchalance was ruined when she shrugged and almost spilled the contents of her cup onto her dress.

"You didn't notice?" Lang shook her head. "What am I going to do with you?" She refused to believe that Pauline enjoyed the independence of being single. For Lang, family was everything.

Face flaming, Pauline ducked her head. "I noticed," she admitted, annoyed at her inability to lie convincingly.

She was—quite literally—saved by the bell when the front door opened to admit Harriet Tuttle, president of the needlework guild, matriarch of local society and self-appointed keeper of the town's morals.

Immediately Lang got to her feet. "Good morning, Harriet," she said with a polite smile.

Harriet acknowledged the Vietnamese woman with a chilly nod before switching her attention to Pauline. Behind Harriet's back, Lang rolled her eyes.

"I must get back," Lang said.

"See you later," Pauline replied before meeting Harriet's beady-eyed stare with her best shopkeeper's smile. "What can I do for you today?"

"I heard that a tree fell onto your carriage house during the storm," Harriet said.

"Bad news travels fast," Pauline replied, wishing the phone would ring. Not only was the older woman one of the worst gossips in town, but her husband was one of the Crescent Cove city council members who would be vetting Pauline's application. "Actually it was a limb that fell, not an entire tree."

Harriet sniffed as though she didn't care to be corrected, even by the primary witness. "Who have you contracted to fix the damage?" she persisted as she glanced around. "Not that Steve Lindstrom, I hope?"

For a moment, Pauline was puzzled by Harriet's apparent hostility. Blond, blue-eyed native resident Steve should fall within her narrow parameters of who was an acceptable member of their community—even though he was divorced, which probably earned him a black mark in her book.

Suddenly Pauline recalled hearing that one of Harriet's sons had recently started his own construction business. Was *that* why she had stopped by—to drum up work for him?

"The repairs are really pretty minor," Pauline explained, fingers crossed behind her back. "My new boarder is actually going to do them."

Harriet's bushy white brows arched above the silver frames of her glasses. Her upper lip curled with scorn, drawing attention to the thin mustache that adorned it.

"You hired a *female* contractor?" As someone who prided herself on knowing everything that went on in the town, she was well aware that Pauline only rented her rooms to women.

Until now, at least.

Before Pauline could reply, Harriet made an irritating tsking sound. "My dear, despite popular opinion, there are certain tasks that women will *never* have the strength or the dexterity to perform as well as men." She patted her own bony chest. "When I was younger, I certainly wouldn't have been interested in using *tools,*" she continued as though the term were something obscene, "or climbing ladders like some sort of monkey from the jungle."

Pauline blinked away the disturbing image that came to mind of Harriet looking like a female Tarzan or wearing a hard hat and safety goggles as she cut through a sheet of plywood with a power saw. Although Pauline abhorred the notion of pounding people into narrow slots like wooden pegs, she couldn't afford to alienate the old crone.

Knowing Harriet would consider it a blemish on Pauline's character if she were to hear the truth from another source, Pauline pretended a calmness she didn't feel. She rearranged some of the thread cutters and clip-on lights in the display case while she debated her options.

"Mr. Garrett is newly returned from California," she finally admitted. "He needed a place to stay, so we worked an agreement."

"Garrett?" Harriet echoed with a frown. "I don't recall that name." She sniffed again. "I certainly hope you know what you're about."

Pauline held on to her temper by reminding herself silently of just how much influence Harriet wielded in this town. Her family, the Barthropes, had been among the first settlers to the area—a fact she never let anyone forget.

Pauline made a noncommittal sound in her throat that she hoped would satisfy the old bat.

"How fortunate that you have the rooms over the carriage house," Harriet continued. "A woman in your position must guard her reputation, *especially* after the unfortunate events in your past."

Pauline nearly choked. Was Harriet referring to her parents' accident or her own broken engagement? Pauline could hardly be held accountable for either of the two most heartbreaking events of her life, but it was obvious that to Harriet they were merely blots on her reputation.

Before Pauline could think of a suitable reply, Harriet leaned forward and tapped her arm. The touch of Harriet's bony fingers sent a shiver up Pauline's spine, but she resisted the urge to retreat.

"If you were to attract any further negative attention," the old woman said with a cool smile, "I would be forced to oppose your application to the city council. After all, a person who sets herself up as an example to others must conduct herself in a manner that is above reproach."

Chapter Three

Bertie straightened her long green dress over her considerable girth. "Don't look now," she muttered under her breath as the front door opened and she grabbed Pauline's arm to prevent her from turning around. "A major hottie just wandered in. Probably got lost looking for Archie's Pub," Bertie added in a loud whisper.

Pauline had a pretty good idea who'd just arrived. She had summoned Bertie as soon as Wade had let her know he'd finished the supply list. Ignoring Pauline's protests, he'd insisted on picking her up here rather than meeting her at Builders' Supply.

Even though Pauline told herself now that she had only given in to his macho demands for the sake of expediency, a knot of anticipation formed in her stomach as she extricated herself from Bertie's loose grasp. What would he think of her little business?

"That's no hottie, it's my new tenant," Pauline replied drily before she pasted on her best welcoming smile. "Hello, Wade," she said, ignoring Bertie's gusty sigh. "I hope you didn't have any trouble finding me."

He removed his sunglasses and hooked them into the neck of his shirt. "No problem. Downtown's where it always was."

His smile stirred a visceral response in Pauline. Silently she agreed with Bertie's comment. If his rangy build and lean, angular face weren't enough to ensure him a spot on the all-time hottie list, the contrast between his black hair and light-gray eyes certainly was.

Ruthlessly she pushed the thought aside as Bertie muffled her giggle behind her hand.

"Bertie, this is Wade Garrett, my new boarder." She stepped aside so the other woman couldn't duck behind her. She knew that Bertie could be extremely shy around strangers because of her size.

"Hi," Bertie murmured, her gaze dropping to the floor.

Instead of dismissing her with a glance, as sometimes happened, his smile widened and he stepped forward. When Bertie, who was barely five feet tall and nearly as wide, glanced back up, he held out his hand.

"Thank you for stepping in so I can borrow your boss for a couple of hours," he told her gravely as he enfolded her hand in both of his.

Before Pauline could protest that their errand shouldn't take that long, Bertie nodded her head like a Bobblehead doll. "She works way too hard."

Wade leaned closer, causing her dark eyes to widen with alarm. "Maybe we can fix that," he said in a conspiratorial tone before releasing her hand. "I invited her to lunch."

Bertie's answering smile transformed her round face. "That's a good start."

"Hey," Pauline protested, "you don't need to talk about me as though I weren't standing right here."

Wade and Bertie exchanged amused glances. "Testy," he observed. "She definitely needs some fresh air."

"Take as long as you want," Bertie said. "I can manage just fine."

Pauline knew she couldn't win against both of them, so she grabbed her purse from behind the counter before they managed to embarrass her further.

When she noticed how intently Wade was looking around, she was tempted to ask if he was a secret stitcher, as she thought of men who hid their needlework hobby. Somehow the image of Wade working a cross-stitch pattern wouldn't quite gel in her mind.

"I'll be back as soon as I can," she told Bertie, making her escape without bothering to see if he was following her.

"Feel better now that you've asserted yourself?" he teased as he reached around her to open the front door.

The amusement in his voice irked her further. "I'll feel better if my garage roof gets repaired before the next storm," she snapped as she headed outside, only to stop abruptly when she realized she had no idea where he'd parked.

"So you're going to be in a bad mood until it's done?" he asked cheerfully as he led the way to his car, which was parked prominently in front of Lang's shop.

Pauline had been about to insist that she wasn't in a bad mood, but then she took a deep breath and reconsidered.

"I'm sorry," she said quickly before getting into his car. "Could we go back and start over?"

He stared down at her, obviously surprised by her abrupt reversal. What an unpleasant woman he must have decided her to be—and who could blame him?

"If we go back, does that mean I'd have to give up this prime parking spot?" he asked.

She was about to ask what he was talking about when she saw the humor lurking in his eyes. "No, not good enough," she said in an equally serious tone. "I'm afraid that really starting over means you have to drive back to San Francisco."

To her surprise, a fleeting frown crossed his face before he smiled and gestured for her to get into his car. "Let's just go on from here," he suggested, leaning down to tuck in the edge of her skirt.

When he shut the door, it occurred to her that she had no idea what he had done in California or why he'd left. Perhaps he *couldn't* return.

A string of possibilities marched through her mind. Was he on the run? A recently released ex-con, ashamed of his past? A grifter in search of his next victim? A car thief? A serial killer?

Oblivious to her dark thoughts, Wade slid behind the wheel, donned his sunglasses and started the engine.

"Which way?" he asked, glancing in his rearview mirror before pulling out.

Reminding herself that Bertie knew where she had gone and with whom, Pauline relaxed against the luxurious leather seat. The instrument panel was made from some exotic wood—real, not some phony laminate—and the carpet beneath her feet was as thick as her neighbor Mrs. O'Connelly's brogue. "Follow Harbor Avenue up the long hill," she directed him. "When you get to the top, you'll see the big sign on the right. Turn into the parking lot."

They rode slowly in silence while he braked for all the jaywalking pedestrians who stepped into the street without looking.

"So you worked construction down in California?" she asked as they drove past the marina.

"I was a partner in an investment firm," he replied after an infinitesimal pause.

She couldn't have been more surprised if he had told her that he used to be an astronaut. Imagining him in a silver space suit was only slightly more difficult than a dress shirt and tie.

"Do you plan to open an office here?" she asked. If a good profile was an indication of noble character, she had no worries. His was positively elegant.

Wade stopped at a red light and glanced at her, but his shades hid his expression. "Don't people in this town invest their money?" he asked. "Or do they just bury it, like pirate booty?"

"For the most part, they work hard for it," she cautioned. "They may not be eager to entrust it to a stranger."

"I'm not a total stranger," he replied. "My grandfather, Morris Garrett, worked in the mill here. When I was a kid, I came up to see him a couple of times during summer vacation." He accelerated when the light turned green. "I've been seriously considering a career change, though, so it may not matter."

"If you become a full-time handyman, you'll have to trade your car in for a pickup truck with oversize tires and a toolbox in the back," she teased, expecting him to deny the idea.

His expression was unreadable. "I've learned that giving up material goods isn't that difficult," he said enigmatically before slowing for the turn into Builders' Supply. "Is this place always so busy?"

Even though his previous comment stirred her curiosity, she had no choice but to go along with the change of subject. To do otherwise would invite him to return the favor and question her about things she would rather not discuss.

"Restoring the old Victorians has gotten quite popular," she said as they drove down the row. "Some of them sell for over a million dollars."

"Have you ever considered selling your house?" he asked as he slid into an empty spot. "Maintaining a place like that must be a lot of work." Perhaps he was thinking about going into real estate.

"No, I would never consider selling Mayfield Manor," she replied, unfastening her seat belt. "Someday I hope to finish the renovation that my mother started."

"A noble ambition," he said as they walked together toward the entrance.

As they passed the outdoor display of plant pots and barbecues, Pauline spotted a big man with shaggy blond hair coming straight toward them.

"Hi, Steve," she said. "I should have known you'd be hanging out here."

"Hey, doll," he replied with a grin and a questioning glance at Wade. "Did the tarp hold okay?"

"Yes, thanks." She glanced back at Wade, who was hanging back. "Steve Lindstrom, Wade Garrett," she recited with appropriate gestures.

The two men exchanged wary nods, hands remaining firmly in their pockets.

"Sorry I haven't finished writing up your bid," Steve told her. "Since the last storm, I've been slammed. The price of lumber's shot up like a rocket, too, so I've had to recalculate everything."

"Wade's going to do the repairs for me," she replied.

"Oh?" Steve's gaze sharpened as he took the other man's measure. "I haven't seen you around, Garrett."

"Wade's from California," Pauline explained hastily. "He's staying at the house, so we made a deal."

Steve's eyebrows shot up. "I see," he drawled knowingly.

A muscle jumped in Wade's cheek, but he remained silent. Pauline refused to justify herself in front of an audience, but she was beginning to feel as though she should have cards printed up.

It's just business.

"Well, let me know if you need any help," Steve said with a nod at Wade. "Garrett."

"Lindstrom," Wade replied gravely.

"Thanks, Steve," Pauline said, marveling at the male protocol, so different from that of her own sex.

"Steve's the contractor I originally thought you worked for," she explained once he was out of earshot.

"Oh, the *contractor,*" Wade echoed, snapping his fingers. "I guess his attitude had me fooled."

"What do you mean?" she asked as she led the way into the store.

"He seemed a little territorial," he replied. "As in, personal relationship."

His comment caught her off guard and she didn't even think about it being none of his business. "I've known him forever, but I don't rob cradles," she protested. "He was two years behind me in school and he dated my sister, so that makes him kind of a surrogate brother." For some reason she didn't fully understand, she wanted Wade to know that she wasn't interested in Steve romantically.

"Good to know," Wade murmured.

She didn't bother to puzzle out his comment as she reached the door to the store manager's office. "I'll see about opening an account," she said instead. "Where should I meet you?"

He glanced around. "I'll be over in roofing."

As Wade walked away from his landlady-slash-boss, he reminded himself that he wasn't doing half bad after a shaky start with Wallingford and his damned lease. Wade had shelter and work to keep him occupied, while the truck with the rest of his stuff would be here this afternoon. So what was his problem?

It certainly didn't have anything to do with meeting Pauline's friend, Steve-o, or the fact that he'd called her "doll," as if they had something going despite her protest to the contrary. When had Wade become afraid of a little competition when it came to a woman who interested him?

Perhaps it had begun with his castration back in Frisco. Apparently Sharon had cut off more than the obvious, but that was going to change.

By the time Pauline caught up with Wade a little while later, he'd found everything on his supply list.

"Sorry I took so long," she said, slightly out of breath. "I ran into a customer from the shop who was here with her husband. They were picking out paint colors for their living room and I couldn't get away from them."

"No problem," he replied, amused by her obvious agitation. "I ordered everything I need to start the job. It will be delivered in the morning."

"That's great." Her face lost its anxious appearance. "Where's the invoice?"

The young clerk who had been helping Wade stepped forward. "I just printed it up for your husband, ma'am. All I need is a signature."

Wade took the form. "Did you want to check it over first, *sweetheart?*" he asked Pauline with a lecherous grin.

She batted her eyes at him coyly. "Why, yes, *honey*. I know how crazy you can get when it comes to remodeling projects." She turned to the clerk, who looked distinctly uncomfortable. "You should see our garage," she confided. "I swear the man owns every power tool on the market."

Wade rested his hand on her shoulder possessively. "Believe me, my tools don't compare to her antique doorknob collection. I swear I should buy stock in eBay, for all the time and money the little woman spends there."

Pauline sent him a look that promised retribution. "I think we've wasted enough of this poor man's time, sugar buns. If I could just peek at the invoice, we could all move on."

Wondering whether she intended to question each item, Wade handed it over. Quickly she skimmed the list before signing the bottom.

"Thank you for keeping him from buying out the store," Pauline told the young clerk. "Sometimes it's like a sickness. He can't seem to help himself."

"Yes, ma'am." He was careful not to look at Wade, who was having trouble keeping a straight face. "Have a nice day, and good luck with your doorknobs."

Wade couldn't resist leaning closer. "Come on, baby cakes," he murmured, breath tickling her ear. "Let's get some lunch."

Pauline had meant to insist that he take her straight back to the shop, but instead she found herself seated across from him at a small seafood place by the marina. It was barely more than a shack, but the food was good and the booths were comfortable.

After they seated themselves, he removed his sunglasses and set them on the scarred table. "What's good here?" he asked as he turned over the laminated card that served as a menu.

Pauline didn't bother looking at hers. "Everything," she replied, realizing she was starved. "But my favorite is the fish chowder. It's never the same, but it's always delicious."

A young waitress she didn't recognize came over to take their orders. She was wearing a pink uniform with a short skirt and thick-soled white shoes that squeaked when she walked.

"What can I bring ya?" she asked, jaws working a wad of gum as she pulled a pencil and pad from her apron pocket. Her eyebrow was pierced with a small silver hoop and an elaborate tattoo circled one thin wrist in stark contrast to her outfit.

"I'll have a cup of the chowder, a Caesar side salad and iced tea," Pauline replied.

"Same here," Wade chimed in. "But bring me a bowl of the chowder instead of a cup."

"A *doorknob* collection?" Pauline demanded after the waitress had left. "Couldn't you come up with anything a little less nerdy? Antique snuffboxes or African art maybe."

He shrugged helplessly. "I saw a display behind you," he said without a hint of apology. "Could have been worse."

"Yes, I'm fortunate that we weren't standing in the plumbing department," she agreed as the waitress brought their iced teas.

Wade's appreciative chuckle made her feel extremely clever.

"Speaking of tools," he said after he'd dumped two packets of sugar into his glass and stirred it energetically, "I'm meeting the guy with my stuff in front of the Safeway store at three, so I'll be ready to start ripping off the old material in the morning." He drank some tea. "Oh," he added, "I ordered a Dumpster. It'll be delivered this afternoon."

Pauline tore her gaze from his tanned throat. Carefully she picked the seeds from her lemon wedge before plopping it back into her glass. "Good idea. Did you rent a storage unit for your things?" He probably owned a lot of fancy furniture and sports equipment. Judging from the long, ropy muscles in his arms, he certainly didn't look like someone who sat around playing video games on his computer and eating snack chips.

"Sure did," he replied. "That place by the courthouse seemed reasonable, and there's decent security."

"So you're planning to stay in Crescent Cove for a while?" she probed gently.

"If things work out," he said enigmatically.

She doubted he was referring to the repairs to her roof, but she resisted the urge to ask. Experience had taught her that asking personal questions invited the same in return. He would hear the gossip soon enough.

The waitress set down their salads, returning immediately with their chowder and a basket of individually wrapped crackers. "Anything else?" she asked, chewing her gum as though she were beating eggs.

When they both shook their heads, she tore their check from her pad and slapped it down between them. "You can pay up front."

Pauline reached for the check, but Wade beat her. "My invitation, my treat," he said, waving it triumphantly.

"It's not a date," she protested, nipping it from his hand. "It's just part of doing business."

He tipped his head to the side as he studied her, his perusal making her uncomfortable. Perhaps she should let him pay.

"What would constitute a date in your estimation?" he asked, sprinkling pepper onto his salad.

She considered the question carefully as she leaned forward to inhale the steam from her chowder. "A date is a social occasion that normally takes place between two people who want to get to know each other better."

Lord, she sounded as prissy as an old spinster reciting from a Victorian social guide for the corset-prone.

"Hmm." Wearing a thoughtful expression, Wade began eating.

"What do you mean, *hmm?*" she demanded, unable to help herself.

He chewed and swallowed with a maddening lack of haste, his gaze never wavering from her face. Finally, feeling self-conscious, she began picking at her salad.

"Using your definition, are you dating anyone at the moment?" he asked.

The unexpected question flustered her. "That's rather personal, don't you think?"

Wade unwrapped a little packet of crackers. "I'm new around here, remember? I'm not prying. I'm trying to get to know the locals."

She had no idea how that related to her dating status, but the current dry spell in her social life was no dark secret. "No, I'm not seeing anyone at the moment," she replied. "What about you? Will your family be joining you?"

He shook his head. "I'm divorced, no kids."

She waited for him to continue, but he resumed eating.

"I'm sorry," she murmured, nearly stumbling on the lie. She was surprised that her nose didn't grow like Pinocchio's, but she would streak downtown naked before she would admit that his single status was good news. "Was it recent?" she ventured.

His eyes seemed to ice over and a muscle twitched in his cheek, so she was surprised when he answered. "Nearly a year. Have you ever been married?"

Turnabout was fair play, and it served her right for being nosy. "Not quite," she admitted, dismayed that the subject could still tighten a knot in her stomach well over a decade after the fact. "I was engaged once, but it didn't work out." What an understatement! Carter Black had changed her life.

"My turn to say sorry," Wade said, distracting her from the past, "but I don't think I'll bother."

Still pushing aside the bad memories, she wasn't sure what he meant, but she realized it was time for a change of subject.

Before she could come up with something totally innocuous, he spoke again.

"What's it like to grow up in a small town with the same bunch of people?" he asked. "Is it boring or comfortable?"

She took a sip of her iced tea. "A little of both, I guess," she replied, exchanging waves with two men she knew slightly when they came into the café.

Wade glanced over his shoulder before turning back to Pauline. "Is it true that you all know everyone else's business?"

Her smile felt forced. "People gossip, just like they do anywhere, but I don't think it's worse than anywhere else." It's only the scandals that people remember, she wanted to add, like when you catch your fiancé kissing another woman. "I take it you didn't grow up in a small town?" she asked instead.

He set aside his empty soup bowl. "Me? No, not unless you call Sacramento a small town. We moved around when I was a kid, but always in that same area."

"That must have been difficult," she replied as she glanced at her watch, shocked to see how much time had passed since she'd left the shop. "Always being the new kid."

He ran a hand over his short hair. "No kidding. I'll bet Steve was a jock, though. What did he play, football?"

"What do you have against jocks?" she asked curiously. "You probably played sports in school." Wade certainly looked athletic, with his rangy build and muscular arms.

To her surprise, he chuckled, a nice, masculine sound. "I was a real geek in high school," he admitted. "Member of the math club, president of the science club. But it was always the athletes who got the babes. You know, the guys with lettermen's jackets and no necks."

An image flashed across Pauline's mind of Lily and Steve on her prom night, a golden princess in a long pink dress on the arm of her broad-shouldered prince in his rented tux.

Lily, what happened? She wondered silently. *You seemed to be so much in love with each other.*

It sure as heck wasn't the first time that Pauline had been totally wrong about that emotion, but she didn't plan to make the same mistake again.

"I can't picture you as a geek," she blurted.

"I'll take that as a compliment," Wade drawled, his smile widening. "Back then, I was skinny and uncoordinated, with a tendency to stammer whenever I tried talking to girls, which wasn't often. How about you? I'll bet you were in the popular crowd."

"No, my sister was the pretty one." Pauline fiddled with her straw. "I was a brain, a girl geek, I guess you could say."

The intensity of his gaze made her uncomfortable. "Your sister must be something if she's prettier than you," he said gallantly.

She made a production of checking her watch again. "I really should get back to work."

"Yeah, me, too. I've got a couple of things to do before Frank gets up here with the truck." He slid from the booth without even trying to wrestle the check from her and donned his sunglasses. "Thanks for lunch. I'll wait for you outside."

"You all come back soon," the waitress told Pauline after she had paid for their meal and added a generous tip. "Enjoy the afternoon."

Wade was leaning against his car, watching an older couple casting lines off their sailboat. When Pauline approached him, her footsteps crunching on the crushed shells of the parking lot, he straightened.

"You look as though you'd like to join them," she observed as he held open the passenger door for her. "Do you have a boat?"

"No," he replied with a wry expression. "John, my business partner, had a thirty-foot sloop that we took out together, so it never made sense for me to buy a boat of my own." After carefully shutting her door, he walked around the car and slid behind the wheel.

"Do you sail?" he asked.

A cold, greasy feeling of dread slid through her stomach. "No, I don't like being on the water." Swallowing hard, she smoothed her skirt over her knees and clutched her purse tightly as he turned the key in the ignition.

He glanced at her but didn't comment.

"You must miss John," she said, steering the conversation away from herself. "Is he still down there?"

This time there was an edge to Wade's smile. "He left Frisco before I did. Now the poor guy is stuck in Avenal, and I've been too busy moving to give him much thought."

That sounded a little cold, but perhaps the two men weren't as close as Pauline had assumed. There must be some reason—more than career burnout—for Wade to move so far away.

"I've never heard of Avenal," she said as she smoothed the wrinkles from her linen skirt. "Is it pretty small?"

The sheriff passed them, headed in the opposite direction, as Wade's smile widened for an instant and then disappeared. "It's a little town between Fresno and Santa Barbara. Not much there except a prison."

It certainly didn't sound like a good location for someone who handled finances, but maybe John had changed careers, too.

"Ever been to Disneyland?" he asked, slowing behind a rusty old camper with aluminum lawn chairs bungee-corded to the back above a half-dozen faded bumper stickers.

"Just once when I was little." She pushed the bittersweet memories away before they could sadden her. "You?"

"A few times," he replied as they approached her block.

"You can let me off right there." She pointed at a loading zone across the street from her shop.

After he complied, his gaze met hers. "Thanks for lunch."

"Thanks for picking me up." She opened her door so he wouldn't feel the need to get out of the car. "See you later."

There was a break in the steady line of traffic, so she hurried across the street. When she reached the curb and turned to wave, he was already driving away.

Pauline was left with a batch of unanswered questions and the growing suspicion that there was more to Wade's past then he cared to admit.

Chapter Four

The next morning Wade began tearing off the ruined shakes and dropping them into the Dumpster beside the garage. He could tell that the roof had been replaced at some point in the past. The house was similar in style to some of the Victorians in San Francisco known as the Painted Ladies.

His grandfather had told him about the economic boom back in the late 1890s, before the railroad had gone bankrupt and Crescent Cove was plunged into a recession. He had explained how the economic downturn had helped preserve so many of the historic buildings because there had been no reason to replace them.

Wade took a break from the hard, dirty work when the truck delivered the new materials he'd ordered. Despite the occasional breeze that blew in from the water, heat radiated off the roof as it would from a cast-iron skillet. It made him feel like a human pork chop. Perhaps he should have tried harder to find another place to stay before agreeing to this arrangement, he chided himself as he stretched the kinks out of his aching back and wiped the sweat that dripped into his eyes.

Especially when he had no idea whether the reason behind his decision returned his interest or not. She was damned hard to read.

After his delivery was unloaded and he had signed for it, he took a long drink from the garden hose and then ducked his head under the icy flow of water. Gasping, he straightened and shook off the excess water like a dog. Once his vision was clear again, he shut off the outdoor faucet and scrambled back up the ladder.

It was a good thing that heights had never bothered him, because the second-story addition to the garage put him high enough so that falling off the edge wasn't a great option.

The view was fantastic. At the north end of town was the sprawling and still-active lumber mill where his grandfather had worked as a mechanic. Wade could remember him complaining about the grease that was permanently lodged beneath his fingernails and in the creases on his wide palms. Today the smoke rose from the mill's twin stacks as it had for over a century. Gray-and-white gulls glided in circles, searching for food in the water below. Farther out, a giant container ship headed toward Seattle's deep-water port.

Reluctantly Wade turned his attention back to the

problem at his feet. The falling limb had poked holes in the layer of paper that formed a moisture barrier beneath the damaged shakes. He'd hoped the decking would be in good shape, but it, too, had suffered from the blow. The job was going to take longer than he had originally figured. He might have to renegotiate his deal.

After he had cut away the bad paper, pried up the smashed plywood and dragged it all to the edge of the roof so he could drop it directly into the Dumpster below, he sat down carefully. With one leg dangling over the side, he tipped his face toward the sun, eyes closed, and planned out the next step.

The sound of tires crunching on the gravel distracted him. A truck had turned into the driveway, but its windshield reflected the light like a mirror, so he couldn't see the driver. Curious, he braced one arm on his bent knee and watched while a man in work clothes emerged.

As soon as he looked up, Wade recognized Steve Lindstrom from the Builders' Supply parking lot.

"Hey, Garrett, how's it going?" he called up to Wade, the brim of his cap shading his face.

"Good," Wade replied. "The worst is done."

Lindstrom glanced over at the half-full Dumpster. "Yeah, I hate tear-outs 'cause you never know what you'll find."

"I'm just realizing that," Wade admitted. Taking advantage of the chance to straighten his legs, he shifted around awkwardly and climbed down the ladder. "Are you looking for Pauline?" he asked when he reached the ground. "She's probably still at the shop."

"Nah, I finished up my job a little early, so I thought I'd see if you needed any help," Steve replied, hands braced on his hips. "I've got my tools and a couple of free hours, if you're interested."

His offer caught Wade by surprise, but then he remembered that Steve and Pauline were friends and this was still basically a small town. "Sure thing." Wade wasn't about to run off a willing worker, especially one as obviously experienced as Steve.

As Wade turned back toward the garage, Steve clapped him on the shoulder. "First let me buy you the best burger this side of Port Angeles. I can't work on an empty stomach, and neither should you."

Wade's first thought was to speculate whether Steve planned to put him on notice about Pauline. His second that it would be a chance to ask a few questions of his own. Was there a reason that such a sharp, attractive woman didn't appear to be involved with anyone? Or did she have something going that she didn't broadcast?

"I'd like to get the plywood installed today so I don't have to put the tarp back up." Wade jerked a thumb toward the upstairs apartment. "The bathroom ceiling collapsed into the tub, and the floor by the toilet shows some ongoing rot. It's probably been leaking around the wax ring for a while."

"I saw how much rain had gotten in during the storm," Steve replied. He opened the door of his truck and slid behind the wheel. "We'll get the food to go if you want," he offered through the open passenger window.

Wade's stomach chose that moment to emit a low, hollow growl that sent his last reservation into oblivion.

Steve was right—a man had to eat. He unfastened his tool belt and laid it aside.

Steve shifted a clipboard from the passenger seat to the floor. "Sorry about the mess," he said with an unrepentant grin. When he started the engine, the driving beat of a classic Shania Twain song poured from the speakers. "What a voice," he said admiringly as he lowered the volume.

"Who cares if she can sing," Wade commented, glancing at the photo on the CD case. He cranked the volume halfway back up, tapping his fingers along with the beat.

Steve nodded in obvious agreement as he backed out of the driveway. "I hear you."

"Did you get a lot of work from the storm?" Wade asked between songs as they drove down the hill toward the bay. The air through the open window felt good against his face. He rubbed his hand over his short hair, glad it didn't brush his neck like Steve's.

Steve braked at the stop sign. "I did some small repairs for a few old customers, but I've pretty much switched from remodeling houses to building them."

"How are home sales around here?" Wade asked, his nose for investments beginning to twitch.

"It's a growing market." Steve cruised past a tavern and a couple of old warehouses, then turned into a crowded parking lot. Right in the middle sat a squat, small building with peeling white paint. Burger Shack read a faded sign mounted on the flat roof. Several overflowing trash cans were scattered around the lot.

"Don't let the appearance fool you," Steve cautioned as they bumped across the patched, uneven asphalt.

"Does the health department know about this?" Wade asked.

"Where do you think they all eat?" Steve drawled as he pulled up next to a big board with a speaker and a flyspecked menu. The little shack was too small for inside seating, but there were a few plastic tables and chairs scattered on one side of it, all full.

"What do you want?" Steve asked. "My treat."

"Thanks, I think," Wade joked, glancing at the menu.

Steve pushed the button under the rusted speaker. After they gave their order to the disembodied voice that crackled with static, he pulled up behind an old beater waiting at the window. The truck's tailgate was missing and the bed was filled with rakes, shovels, a couple of lawn mowers and a sack of fertilizer. Three guys were crammed into the cab.

"Do you buy lunch for every newcomer in town?" Wade asked Steve.

"No way. And I'm not coming on to you, either," he said with a wink. "I'm as straight as an arrow."

"What, you feel a need to point that out because I'm from San Francisco?" Wade asked.

Steve's grin faded and he flushed as red as a bad sunburn. "Hey, no, uh, I'm sorry," he stammered, extending his hand and then quickly snatching it back. "Look, I didn't mean any offense, honest," he added while Wade watched in silent amusement. "I didn't think... I mean, it doesn't matter if you're... I was just kidding, really." Steve shook his head, staring at the wheel. "Crap," he muttered under his breath.

He looked so thoroughly embarrassed that Wade burst out laughing, just as the pickup in front of them drove away with its gears grinding.

Steve's head snapped up. For a moment, he stared hard at Wade and then he, too, began to laugh.

"You dog!" He punched Wade's shoulder as he braked at the pickup window.

"Nice apology, though," Wade commented, still chuckling. No way was he going to give in and rub his aching arm. "A little rough on the delivery, but I'd give it a nine for sincerity."

"I owe you, Garrett." Steve's tone was cheerful as he passed bags of food and drinks to Wade.

"Bring it on," he replied as Steve dug out his wallet.

An older man wearing whites bent down to hand back the change. "Hey, Steve," he exclaimed with a nod at Wade. "When are you gonna build me a house?"

"When are you going to part with your secret barbecue recipe?" Steve countered.

"No can do. I'm willing it to my kids," the man said with a final wave.

"Nice guy," Steve said as they drove away. "The whole family works there. You'd never know it from looking at Pete's ugly mug, but he's got three daughters—all redheads—and any one of them could stop traffic on Highway 101 without breaking a sweat." He kissed his fingertips as an Italian chef would. "*Bella.*"

Wade shook his head as he resisted the urge to raid

the bags on his lap. "You got a particular fondness for redheads?" he asked.

"Two of them are a little young, and the other one just got engaged. Pete blames them for his gray hair."

He inhaled deeply. "I can't wait," he groaned, pulling up by a fishing pier. "Let's eat."

Shuffling bags, they dived in.

"All we need to make this perfect is a cold six-pack," Steve mumbled, mouth full.

"Uh-huh." Wade tossed a fat, greasy fry to a waiting gull while he chewed and swallowed his first massive bite of burger. "If you've got something going with the lady of the manor, just tell me and I'll steer clear, I swear."

Burger poised, Steve frowned, appearing genuinely puzzled. "If I what? Who did you say?"

It was Wade's turn to feel his cheeks heat up as he realized what he had nearly revealed. "Dolly?" he bluffed.

Steve's eyes widened with comprehension. "Are you asking if I'm interested in *Pauline?*" His tone was so incredulous that she would surely have taken offense if she'd been here.

"Uh, yeah," Wade admitted, grabbing his soda. "She's not bad-looking, and you made such a point of letting me know that you're not gay." He glanced at Steve's bare left hand. "Or maybe you aren't single."

"Hey, I'm extremely single and I like girls just fine," Steve blustered, sprinkling salt on his fries. "But Pauline is like a big sister, and the idea of hooking up with her is a little too, um, incestuous, if you want the truth."

The tenseness in Wade's shoulders let loose as though a string had been cut. "Are you two related?"

he asked before taking another big bite. Steve was right about the burger. It was thick and tasty, with juice dripping into the wrapper.

"Only in the sense that her sister and I had a thing going for a while back in school." Steve's voice had gone flat, his face expressionless except for the jaw muscle that twitched.

"Does she still live around here?" Wade asked curiously.

Steve tore open a ketchup packet with his teeth. "Nope."

When he didn't elaborate, Wade got the message. "So is there a good place in town for a guy to get a beer and a friendly game of pool?" he asked.

Steve's grin flashed again. "How friendly do you have in mind?"

Wade took a long swig of soda while he pondered his answer. "Couple bucks a game, maybe, just to keep it interesting." He gazed out the windshield as a red convertible zoomed by with a blonde behind the wheel. "Unless that's too rich," he challenged.

Steve's answering grin bared his teeth. "Make it five and you're on."

"Yeah, I guess I could manage that," Wade said, injecting hesitation into his voice.

"The Crab Pot's got good tables, if you aren't hung up on am-bi-ence," Steve replied, emphasizing each syllable. "Pool tourney every Wednesday night." He pointed up the road. "Just follow Beach Drive past the sawmill and you can't miss it."

"Thanks. Maybe I'll check it out." Wade wiped his

mouth with a paper napkin. "Well, I'd better get back. You still want to help?"

Steve glanced at the dashboard clock as he started the engine. "Damn straight."

When Pauline got home from work, she was surprised to see Wade still at work on the roof and new plywood covering a large area. Surrounded by bundles of raw cedar shingles, he was on his hands and knees spreading out a roll of tar paper. Since he gave no indication of having noticed her arrival, she allowed herself a moment's indulgence to study him.

As he reached for his hammer, his T-shirt rode up to reveal a line of tanned skin on his back above the gaping waistband of his jeans. The soft denim hugged his compact rear like a coat of faded paint below his wide leather tool belt.

Awareness sizzled through her, followed by a shiver of caution. A man like him bore a warning label as clearly as if he'd had *Danger* embroidered across his butt in red silk floss.

"Do something for you?" he called out, interrupting her musing.

She hadn't noticed that he had turned to watch her over his shoulder, but now his grin was smug.

She had been wrong about one thing. Being strongly attracted to him wasn't the worst thing that could happen; having him *know* it was.

"You got a lot done today," she called up to him, shading her eyes with her hand. "I guess maybe you do know what you're doing after all."

"Shame on you for doubting me." He stuck the hammer into a loop on his belt and made his way toward the bottom of the steep incline, while she enjoyed the view of his rear end.

"Nice to know I was wrong," she replied, holding her breath while he swung his leg onto the ladder and finally planted both feet safely on the rungs.

"I had no idea it was getting so late until I heard you come down the drive," he said, descending with the sure-footed ease of an oversize monkey.

Hold on to that image, she urged herself silently. "It's nearly time to eat," she informed him. Although she had no real reason to stand around, her feet seemed reluctant to carry her away.

He stepped onto the ground beside her and stripped off his work gloves. A hint of beard shadow blurred the line of his jaw, the stubble adding to his rugged appeal as he unbuckled his work belt.

"Did you sell lots of thread today, Miss Pauline?" he asked softly.

"More than enough to pay what you're worth, Mr. Garrett," she blurted.

When he threw back his head and roared with laughter, she tore her gaze away from the sight of his tanned throat. Even though she felt a burst of embarrassed delight for amusing him, she was able to hide her smile.

"I'm not totally responsible," he said. "Your buddy dropped by to lend a hand."

"Steve was here? I guess that doesn't surprise me."

He opened the side door to the garage so he could leave his tools there. "Yeah, he seems like a good guy.

He bought me lunch at a place called the Burger Shack."

"Did you see the sisters with the red hair?"

Wade scratched his chin. "I missed out. What are they, some kind of local wonder?"

"Pretty much," she replied, walking toward the house. "The Shack has been there for as long as I can remember." She could picture stopping there after a Sunday drive with her parents when she and Lily were small.

The gate to the backyard hung open, but she didn't mention the small omission. She was proud of the shaded oasis she'd created, the deadheaded rhodies and azaleas sprouting new growth while a profusion of asters, carnations, Canterbury bells and peonies filled the flower beds with color. Phlox, tall foxglove and old-fashioned snapdragons waited their turn from behind. A Victorian gazing ball gleamed softly among the ferns, and a concrete birdbath near the redbrick patio had attracted a trio of brightly-colored gold-finches.

Briefly Pauline considered suggesting that they all eat dinner at the white wrought-iron table and matching chairs on the patio if the evening wouldn't be too chilly for Dolly.

"I'll see you inside," Pauline told Wade, who was picking through the supplies stacked by the garage. "Dolly planned to fix a tuna salad for dinner, and I'm sure she made enough for everyone."

He mopped the side of his neck with a handkerchief. "I need a shower before I eat."

Pauline decided she wouldn't mind taking a few minutes to change out of her tailored blouse and slim skirt. Her new sandals had raised a blister on one heel. Why did the choice between comfort and fashionable footwear have to be so difficult for women, when men didn't have that dilemma? They could wear tennis shoes with everything short of a tuxedo—and sometimes even then.

When she reached the foyer, she was startled to see a strange man coming down the stairs with two suitcases.

"What's going on?" she demanded. "What are you doing?"

He froze as Dolly appeared on the landing dressed in a dark-blue pantsuit that she normally wore to church. "I'm so glad you're home," she exclaimed as she came down the stairs. "I didn't want to bother you at the shop or leave a message with Wade."

"Are you going somewhere?" Pauline asked, puzzled. She noticed a taxi parked on the street.

"My older sister down in Portland fell and broke her hip." Dolly stopped with her hand on the banister. "I don't think she would have said anything to me about it, but the hospital refused to send her home without someone to care for her."

"I'm sorry to hear that." Pauline remembered Dolly saying that her sister was older by several years. "I hope she'll be better soon."

The sound of the back door opening and shutting was followed by Wade's footsteps on the kitchen floor. A moment later he appeared in the arched dining room doorway. "Is everything all right?"

Dolly fiddled with the strap of her purse. "I was just telling Pauline that my sister hurt herself, so she needs me to stay with her down in Portland."

"How are you getting there?" he asked, appearing genuinely concerned.

"I'll take the Amtrak from Seattle," she replied. "I've done it before."

"How long will you be gone?" Pauline realized how much she had selfishly counted on Dolly as a buffer with Wade here. At least the other new boarder was scheduled to arrive the day after tomorrow. Pauline hadn't actually met the woman, but she sounded nice enough on the phone and her deposit check hadn't bounced. The money had gone straight into Pauline's savings.

"How long I'm gone will depend on how quickly Irene regains her mobility," Dolly replied. "But I definitely have to be back here before my cruise next month." She checked the contents of her bag. "I'm sorry to do this without more notice—"

"Don't give it a thought," Pauline assured her quickly.

"Is there anything we can do?" Wade asked. "Do you have enough cash?"

Dolly reached up to pat his cheek. "You're a sweetheart to offer. Would you mind watering the plants in my room?"

"No problem," he promised. "I'll treat them like my own."

The cabbie had gone outside with her bags and now he tapped his horn.

Dolly glanced toward the open door. "Oh, dear. I'd better go so I don't miss the ferry. You know how the traffic can back up on the other side."

After she hugged both of them and promised to call as soon as she arrived at her sister's house, she hurried down the front steps and got into the cab.

Pauline and Wade waved from the porch. When they went back into the house, she glanced at him uneasily, wondering if he, too, felt the sudden awkwardness between them.

"Give me ten minutes to shower and then I'll set the table," he said easily, as though the two of them had eaten together a hundred times before.

"Uh, sure," she stammered, watching him bound up the stairs. All of a sudden, the big house didn't seem nearly as spacious as it had before Dolly's departure.

Pauline followed at a much slower pace as she pictured him sleeping right down the hall. If she didn't watch herself, she'd be wondering what, if anything, he wore to bed.

Her imagination wasn't helped by the faint sound of shower water running through the old pipes. Her own shower had better be a cold one.

Wade glanced at his landlady seated across from him as they dined on Dolly's tuna salad and homemade rolls. He didn't need to ask why Pauline had chosen to eat in the dining room instead of the kitchen, which was certainly more convenient as well as being far less intimidating.

It was obvious that she wished to maintain some

illusion of formality. He considered himself lucky that she hadn't seated them at opposite ends of the long table, where they would have needed a shuttle to pass the salt and pepper.

He wished he was better able to decipher what Pauline was thinking. Most of the women he'd known had enjoyed talking about themselves, but when he asked her questions, she usually answered as briefly as possible. Her reticence was beginning to make him wish he had pumped Dolly for information before she'd left.

He was about to ask Pauline to pass the salt when the cordless phone—so out of place on the elaborately carved sideboard—jangled abruptly.

"I'd better get that," Pauline murmured, setting aside her napkin. "It might be Dolly."

Wade glanced at the wall clock. "She can't have arrived yet unless she took a bullet train."

"I hope there isn't a problem," Pauline replied. "You never know with Amtrak."

When she picked up the receiver, Wade listened shamelessly to her side of the conversation. From her growing dismay, he could tell that the caller wasn't Dolly and the news wasn't welcome.

Curious, he helped himself to another roll.

"Are you sure?" Pauline asked the caller. "You've definitely changed your mind?" She appeared to listen intently. "Yes, of course I understand, but I won't be able to refund your deposit."

Wade stopped pretending to butter his roll in order to give her his full attention. After she said goodbye, she replaced the receiver and sat back down with a thump.

"A problem?" he asked as she let out a sigh.

"That was the boarder I expected to arrive the day after tomorrow." Pauline tucked a strand of hair behind her ear. "Her plans have changed, so she's not coming at all."

"I guess we'll have to make the best of the situation," Wade said cheerfully. The prospect of spending time with Pauline was hardly an unpleasant one.

From her expression, she wasn't looking forward to it with quite the same degree of enthusiasm as he. "I was afraid of something like this happening," she muttered. "Now what are we going to do?"

Several suggestions leaped immediately to his mind, but he didn't voice them. "I hope I can count on you to behave yourself," he said instead, hoping to put her at ease with a little levity.

For an instant she appeared startled, but then she rolled her eyes. "Very funny."

"We're adults," he said. "I pick up after myself and I don't mind helping with the chores, so I think we'll do just fine."

She was already shaking her head. "You don't understand. Crescent Cove is a small town and people talk."

"Ignore them. That's what I plan on doing." He wasn't about to admit that he had survived much worse, but neither was he willing to relocate when he had barely unpacked.

She didn't appear convinced.

"This is the twenty-first century, not the nineteenth, and we don't need a chaperone," he added as he speared a slice of hard-boiled egg from his salad.

He was a decent guy. As she got to know him better, she would quit worrying.

"You can't stay here," she said bluntly.

When he glanced up to see her set expression, he nearly dropped his fork. "Excuse me?"

She took a deep breath. "I'm sorry, but the worst gossip in town is the president of the needlework guild that meets at my shop. She's already commented *pointedly* on my having a male boarder, and that was before Dolly left."

"How is this our problem?" he asked, growing impatient. "I don't care about some old harpy's unasked-for opinion and neither should you."

"But I've been working very hard to get appointed to the city council." Her voice rose. "I can't afford a scandal, not even a minor one, before they make their decision."

"Scandal?" Wade echoed, setting down his fork. "Would you listen to yourself! I doubt the city council will jump to any risqué conclusions about our living arrangement, even if they do find out."

"The husband of that harpy I mentioned just happens to be on the city council," she protested. "He's even stuffier than she."

"Good for him." Wade shoved aside his unfinished salad, appetite gone. Pauline appeared near tears, but he refused to be manipulated by the oldest female trick in the book.

The entire conversation was ridiculous. "You told me you'd been engaged, so don't act as though you're a blushing virgin whose reputation has to be protected," he said without thinking.

The shock on her face made him regret his comment. It hadn't been fair.

"I'm sorry. I shouldn't have said that," he apologized, extending his hands, palms up. "I still think you're overreacting. Just because one dried-up old prune made a nosy comment doesn't mean your reputation is going to get trashed. I'm a paying tenant, not some guy you picked up down on the wharf."

Suddenly he remembered his ace in the hole. "I've got a signed lease, remember? Until it expires, you're stuck with me."

The tears swimming in her eyes spilled over. She shoved back her chair and bolted from the dining room. He heard her footsteps on the stairs, followed by the slam of her bedroom door.

In addition to attempting to kick him out, she had also stuck him with the kitchen cleanup.

Chapter Five

Maybe Wade was right, Pauline thought for the hundredth time as she walked the four blocks from her house to the library the next Tuesday afternoon. When she had pulled into her driveway after work and his car hadn't been there, a surge of mingled relief and disappointment had caught her by surprise.

Ever since her melodramatic departure from the dining room the other night, she'd been doing her best to avoid him. The following morning she had taken the coward's way out and left a note giving him a week to make other arrangements. Surely he wouldn't take her to court over that lease they had signed.

She had kept the shop open late on Saturday and all day Sunday to serve the tourists who were in town for the festival weekend. Normally she would have spent her one day off yesterday catching up on chores and resting after the extra-long week. Instead she'd gone to visit a girlfriend in Bremerton. When she'd gotten home that evening, he'd been gone again, so she'd hoped he was looking for a new place to stay.

This morning before she had ventured downstairs, she'd heard him using a nail gun that sounded like a busy woodpecker. He had called out to her when she'd walked to her SUV, but she'd pointed to her watch without stopping.

She couldn't avoid him forever, but right now she was on her way to one of her most important commitments of the week, one that she wasn't willing to cancel.

On Tuesdays she left early and then she kept the shop open late the next night to hold classes on different needlework techniques.

Business had been slow today, giving her plenty of time to reach the reluctant conclusion that Wade had probably been right when he'd said she was overreacting to what her neighbors might think.

Most people had all they could handle in tending to the minutiae of their own lives. Lily's and her fifteen minutes of fame, if one could call it that, had ended a decade ago. Almost everyone who had been around back then had moved away, passed away or just plain forgotten about the incident that had altered Pauline's life and sent her sister into exile.

Relieved to have finally worked out the problem in her mind, Pauline shrugged away the tension that had gripped her shoulders for most of the day. A new burst of energy seemed to propel her along on the short walk to the library.

She still wore her work clothes—a sleeveless coral tank top and cream capri pants. On her feet were comfortable tan sandals that matched her shoulder bag. She was careful not to trip on the uneven patches in the old sidewalk, some of which were badly cracked by the roots of the majestic maple trees that had lined the street for as long as she could remember.

The familiar houses she passed were all relics of the building boom of the late nineteenth century, as was her own home. A few of them were run-down, their neglected exteriors surrounded by weeds and overgrown shrubbery. In one spot she passed, a climbing rosebush with pink blossoms and yellowing leaves seemed to be the only thing holding up a sagging wood fence.

Some of the grand old structures had been lovingly restored to their former glory. As B and Bs or private homes, they would surely rival anything San Francisco had to offer. Several of the larger properties were mainstays on the annual Historical Society walking tour, and she liked to peer through the wrought-iron fences at the velvety green lawns and formal gardens.

Crossing the last street, she approached the double glass doors of the flat-roofed one-story brick building that had replaced the tiny, historic Carnegie Library twenty years ago.

"Hi, Pauline," said the gray-haired clerk at the main desk as she peered over the top of her reading glasses.

Pauline waved without slowing down as she crossed the lobby on her way to the children's room. As always, the particular smell from the shelves full of books welcomed her. Corny as the idea was, she liked to think of it as a potpourri blended from knowledge, adventure and imagination.

As she paused at the water fountain, she wondered if Wade liked to read. She had no idea what he enjoyed doing when he wasn't working with tools. He had watched part of an NBA play-off game on TV but didn't seem particularly obsessed by sports, even though he had mentioned playing pickup basketball. She had no idea whether he owned a computer or laptop or even if he had family somewhere. All she knew was that he was a threat to her carefully ordered world, one that she couldn't afford.

For a good part of her life, the library had been her second classroom, her playground and her refuge from loneliness. Whenever she had been hurt by her parents' obvious preference for her pretty and popular sister, Pauline had found solace in books. For the last five years, ever since she had bought the needlework shop from her former employer, she had conducted an after-school story time—her way of giving back.

As Pauline entered the children's section, she saw Mrs. Coles, the librarian in charge of that department, deep in conversation with a skinny, short-haired girl wearing Goth-style black clothing. When the older woman noticed Pauline, she smiled as she indicated a stack of picture books on her desk.

Pauline scooped them up and headed for the meeting room. Through the glass, she could see that most of the small chairs and floor pillows were already taken. The babble of young voices died as she arrived followed by two more boys and a little girl with curly red hair.

"Hi, kids," Pauline said as she looked around. "It's okay to sit on the carpet if you can't find an empty chair or a pillow."

She gave them all another moment to get settled while she took her seat and glanced through the books that Mrs. Coles had selected. Forgetting about everything else, she selected a classic about a curious monkey. When her audience fell silent in anticipation, she cleared her throat and began to read.

Sometime later, when she finished another story about a talking frog family and closed the cover, the pleading began.

"Don't stop."

"Just one more. Please."

"Read another one!"

Leave 'em wanting more, she thought as she got to her feet. "That's all for today, but I'll be back next week," she promised as she gathered up the books. "Please remember to put your chairs back against the wall and stack the pillows in the corners."

A few mothers and a couple of fathers who had been waiting outside came through the door as a little boy wearing thick glasses began to cry.

After collecting several thank-yous and two hugs, Pauline finally shut the door behind her. She returned the books, but Mrs. Coles was nowhere around, so she checked out a new mystery she'd reserved weeks earlier and went outside.

A volunteer was tucking red-and-white petunias along the sidewalk, which reminded Pauline of the flats of pink geraniums and sapphire-blue lobelia waiting for her to plant in strawberry pots for the front porch. She hadn't given a thought to dinner; perhaps she would order a pizza. If Wade hadn't left for the evening, he would have to fend for himself.

As she walked past the parking lot, she spotted the members of the local literary fiction group arriving for their monthly meeting. Several of the women also belonged to the needlework guild.

Harriet's voice rang out across the parking lot as though she were speaking through a megaphone as she led the group like a tour guide.

"I'm so glad that Oprah decided to read the classics instead of those new books she used to feature," she proclaimed. "To my way of thinking, most of them were entirely too radical to be called 'literature.'"

"I liked that story about the woman who left her abusive husband," said a short woman who was walking quickly to keep up. "She had a lot of courage."

Pauline would have liked to hear Harriet's reply, since she wasn't known for being tolerant of dissenting opinions. Pauline suspected her of being the reason a young Indian woman had dropped out of the guild. The reminder made Pauline shudder as she crossed the street. What would Harriet's reaction be to the news of Dolly's departure?

The old bat had certainly expressed her opinion to

all and sundry thirteen years ago, when Pauline had broken her engagement and Lily had left town abruptly for California. Tongues had wagged for weeks.

Wade could have no way of knowing how much Pauline *loathed* the idea of being talked about behind her back, but she couldn't very well convince him unless she were also willing to discuss a time in her life that she had managed to put behind her. A time when she had merely been "poor Pauline," and not a successful businesswoman being considered for the city council.

For now, she had flowers to plant.

Wade pulled into the driveway and parked beside Pauline's SUV, illuminated by the yard light. He'd meant to stop for one beer while he checked out the place that Steve had recommended. The only problem was that when Wade had walked through the front door of the Crab Pot, Steve had hailed him from a corner booth where he'd been seated with two other guys and a full pitcher of cold beer. He'd insisted that Wade join them.

After answering their questions about the damage to Pauline's garage roof, Wade had sprung for another round as the conversation had drifted back to sports, work and women—not necessarily in that order. He'd been content to sip his beer, observe the locals who wandered in and pretty much let the talk flow around him.

He hadn't realized that Steve had ordered food until the plastic baskets of deep-fried prawns, fish and fries had arrived at the table. It would have been rude for Wade to leave without eating.

Now it was only a little past ten, but he could already see a glow from Pauline's bedroom window. She must have noticed that he hadn't left despite her pissy little note. If she didn't want to know how the repairs were going, he wasn't about to hunt her down. If they didn't talk, they couldn't argue about him moving out.

As he got out of his rig as quietly as possible, the back porch light blinked on. Squinting into the glare, he saw a slight figure peering out at him.

"Who is it?" Pauline called softly in the evening stillness.

Oh, hell, she wouldn't recognize his new wheels. "It's just me," he replied, shifting so she could see him. "Sorry, I didn't mean to alarm you."

Before he could open the gate, she came down the steps, ponytail bobbing, clad in snug-fitting blue sweatpants and a stretchy tank top.

It was the first time he had seen her in anything so revealing, but he'd been right about her figure. She might be slim, but she definitely came equipped with feminine curves.

Dangerous curves. For a moment he forgot all about his new truck.

"Is that yours?" she asked, hands on hips.

Taken aback by her interest, as well as her appearance, he shoved his hands into his pockets and refocused his attention over his shoulder.

"I traded in my car," he admitted quietly so he wouldn't disturb the neighbors beyond the hedge.

"Why?" she asked as she joined him in the driveway, smelling of shampoo and wildflowers.

"I figured a pickup would be more practical up here," he said gruffly.

Even though it was only partly illuminated by the light, she circled it slowly. "It looks big enough to tow a six-horse trailer."

He unlocked the driver's door so she could see the interior. "Now I can haul the materials to finish the garage," he explained as she leaned past him to stick her head into the cab.

"If you're looking for more work, I'm sure Steve would be happy to send some your way," she replied. "He's too busy right now to do basic repair jobs like mine."

Wade stepped back to admire the view of her compact rear in the stretchy fabric of her sweatpants, wondering if she was taunting him deliberately. "Uh-huh."

"It's nice," she said with a last wistful glance as he locked the truck. "I'm envious."

He followed her back to the house, trying to ignore the sway of her hips when she went up the porch steps. Suddenly he found himself longing for a heat wave.

"After I picked up the truck, I ran into Steve and a couple of his buddies at the Crab Pot," he explained when they reached the kitchen.

In the brighter light, he could tell that she wasn't wearing a bra. Her breasts had a nice rounded shape that looked completely natural, and her nipples were clearly visible. Back in California, so many women had undergone some kind of surgical enhancement that he'd quit being impressed by oversize and overshaped racks.

Pauline, on the other hand, was perfect.

"I was going to fix myself a cup of tea," she said, interrupting his silent observation. "Would you like some?"

Her innocent offer bounced around inside Wade's head like a ball in an empty drum. The thirteen-year-old boy inside him wanted to grin like a fool. *Love some*.

"Uh, tea would be great," he stammered like a half-wit, wishing she had offered him a beer instead so he could pour it over his head and be done with it.

Wordlessly she filled the kettle and set it on the stove while he got out mugs and spoons. She offered him a tea bag from a decorated tin, so he selected orange spice and she took lemon. After she had filled both mugs, she sat back down. He braced himself for her to ask when he was moving.

"You probably think that I overreacted," she said instead, staring at her mug.

There wasn't much point in pretending that he didn't know what she meant. "That's true," he admitted cautiously after sipping his tea. Its bland taste reminded him why he preferred coffee, black and rich.

"I've just been so worried about my business and the city council position. But they have to make a decision soon." She removed her tea bag and set it in a flowered dish. "Perhaps Dolly will come back sooner than she figured, like you said."

Not wanting to stir up trouble, he didn't mention the cruise that Dolly had alluded to before she left. "That would certainly settle your dilemma," he agreed.

"Do you miss California?" she asked without looking at him. "To someone like me who's always lived in the same place, it seems like such a huge change."

A few months ago, he would have probably evaded her, but he chose to view her curiosity as a sign that she was interested in getting to know him better. He was tempted to give her the full story, but then he remembered how his friends and business acquaintances had reacted when they'd first heard the news. Even his family doubted him.

"I don't really miss it," he said evasively. "Change can be a positive thing, even an adventure."

She probably thought he was an idiot for throwing away a successful business while she worked so hard to build hers up. Her opinion would really plummet if she knew that he was lucky to not be sitting in a prison cell.

"I find it hard to picture you in a suit and tie," she said, lifting her head so that her gaze met his.

He fought the dizzying impulse to lean over and kiss her soft mouth. "I can't imagine why not," he drawled jokingly as he rubbed his hand over the stubble on his jaw. Not only was he badly in need of a shave, but his hair could stand a trim, since he liked wearing it short. He'd have to ask for a recommendation so that he didn't wander into a beauty salon with a row of humongous dryers and patrons wearing pin curls tinted old-lady blue.

Pauline rewarded his attempt at humor with a faint smile. "Maybe I should be asking you for financial advice instead of help with roof repairs."

"Thanks, but I'll stick to good, honest manual labor for now." He took another swallow of tea that had turned tepid and tried not to show his dislike. He would drink lye if it meant sitting here with her.

She tipped her head, eyes twinkling. "Are you saying your former occupation wasn't honest?"

Wade stiffened, nearly spilling his tea. Had she checked out the real reason he'd left Frisco?

"Are you okay?" Pauline asked. "I was only teasing."

His stunned reaction to her question must have shown on his face. Letting go of the fragile cup before he could break it, he forced himself to relax.

"No problem," he said, smiling as though he hadn't a care in the world. "Actually one of my reasons for coming back to Crescent Cove is that I hope to find out more about an ancestor of mine."

"Oh?" Curiosity lit her features.

His tension eased up. "He was a sea captain whose ship transported lumber from the local mill," he continued. "I'm curious about his life."

"Our library has a wonderful section on local history," she said enthusiastically. "I'm sure you'll find what you need."

She started to push back her chair. Before she could rise, Wade reached out and covered her hand with his.

"Would you help me?" he asked, ignoring her sudden wariness. "Dolly said you spend a lot of time there."

Pauline tugged her hand free. "I read stories to the children," she protested. "That hardly qualifies me as a research assistant. Besides, I'm really busy at work. It's the middle of the tourist season. I'm even behind in my gardening."

He decided to drop the subject for the time being, but he wasn't giving up. If this idea didn't work, he'd figure out some other way to spend time with her.

"I could help with the gardening," he offered. "The grass needs mowing, too."

"The boy who usually does it is away at camp," she replied with a glance at the clock. "Goodness, look at the time! I had no idea it was so late." She popped up from her chair as though she had sat on a spring.

Wade got to his feet. To give his hands something to grab besides her, he took their mugs to the sink. "I'll take care of these," he said, frustrated by her skittishness. "And my offer stands."

Did she return his interest or not? Damned if he knew. Granted, he was no celebrity hunk, but neither was he the monster from the black lagoon. Still, if his instincts were totally off and he made a pass, she would have a solid reason to throw him out.

"Thanks," she said from the doorway. "I'll keep it in mind."

After she left, he put the cups into the dishwasher and then he went to the window to stare out at his truck.

At one time, a new vehicle had been something he took for granted, like a beautiful wife, a successful career and a friendship he could trust. That was before he had learned to value what came his way—a roof over his head, work to keep him occupied and maybe—just maybe—someone who could believe in him, even as he struggled to believe in himself.

Pauline hadn't lied to Wade the other evening when she'd told him the shop kept her occupied. Saturdays were usually the busiest, and today was no exception. From now until the end of the summer, tourists would flood the historic shopping district, eager to buy what the shops offered.

She barely had time to think between customers who'd come, browsed and bought since she'd first unlocked the door. They purchased hand-dyed specialty flosses, linen fabrics and charts that weren't available from the large craft outlets, all tucked into her distinctive yellow bags. A new line of pastel baby bibs and bonnets with fabric inserts ready for cross-stitching nearly flew from their display rack. Customers preferred them over using waste canvas to embroider on regular fabric.

A woman from Vancouver purchased an expensive freestanding wooden needlework frame carved by a local carpenter. Another who was touring the country by motorhome bought every kit with a dog motif that Pauline had in stock.

As usual for a sunny weekend, many of the customers had ridden the ferry from Seattle or driven over the Tacoma Narrows bridge. Some of the people looked familiar, but many told her it was their first time in Crescent Cove.

"Looks like you could use some help," whispered Bertie when she reported to work right before lunch.

Pauline smiled gratefully. "No kidding." She hadn't taken a break all morning, and Lang hadn't shown up, either. As soon as Pauline finished ringing up the latest design book from the Kooler studios, she planned to duck into her tiny back room.

"How's that good-looking roommate of yours?" Bertie asked with a teasing smile and pink cheeks after she had placed the book into a bag and handed it to the customer.

Pauline had already told Bertie about Dolly being called away.

"I imagine that he's fine," Pauline replied under her breath as another woman approached the counter.

"Do you carry any magazines from Great Britain?"

The tone of her voice conveyed her impatience at having to wait.

"Yes, of course," she replied with a smile. "Cross-stitching is very popular over there. Let me show you where they are." Coming around the end of the counter, she led the way, then left the customer to browse.

"I'm going to lunch," she told Bertie. "Holler if you need help."

The other woman waved as she rang up another order. On the way to the office, Pauline stopped twice to answer questions. Finally she entered the small room and shut the door behind her with a sigh of relief. After she had retrieved her sack lunch and a soda from the minuscule refrigerator, she sat at her desk with her feet propped on a shipping carton while she leafed through a new catalog. She had just finished her tuna sandwich when there was a knock on the door.

"Come on in, Bertie," she called out, knowing her assistant wouldn't let a customer invade her sanctum. Munching on a carrot stick, she continued to flip pages. Normally she didn't buy from this supplier, but they had obtained exclusive rights from a designer who sold really well.

When the door opened, she glanced up, startled to see Wade instead of Bertie.

"Working hard, I see," he drawled with his usual devilish grin.

Reaction zinged through her with the force of a lightning bolt as she swung her feet off the box and finished chewing her carrot. "Even the owner gets a chance to eat." She was dismayed by the strength of her attraction. "Is there a problem with the repairs?"

"We need to talk," he replied. Closing the door, he leaned his shoulder against it and hooked one thumb into his leather belt. His presence in the tiny, overcrowded space made Pauline feel positively claustrophobic.

"What's so important that it brought you clear downtown?" she asked. Had he come to tell her he'd found another place to live after all?

His brows arched. "We're not exactly talking L.A. to Vegas here. I could walk it if I had to."

He was right, of course, but she could hardly explain her reaction. She barely understood it herself.

Folding her hands, she gazed up at him expectantly, ignoring how sexy he looked in his work clothes.

"I removed the damaged Sheetrock in the bathroom and there's dry rot in the boards under it," he said. "I'm confident that patching the roof fixed the old leak, but that lumber needs replacing before I can close the wall back up or the rot will spread."

At least the bathroom would be repaired correctly. "Thanks for letting me know," she told him just as there was another knock on the door.

Wade opened it and this time it really was Bertie who

poked in her head. "Sorry to intrude, but apparently a tour bus from Vancouver just unloaded a group of our friends from the north. Word on the street is that it's going to get busy."

"I'll be right there." After Bertie left, Pauline looked back at Wade as she gathered up the trash from her lunch. "Anything else?"

"No, I'll let you get back to work." As soon as he walked away, she ducked into the closet-size restroom, reapplied her lip gloss in front of the tarnished mirror and then hurried out front. Through the window she saw him cross the street as a pretty blonde stared appreciatively.

For the next forty minutes, Pauline didn't have time to think about anything other than ringing up sales. Finally the rush abated as the tour group moved on to the antique stores in the next block.

The next customers who entered the shop were two elderly sisters who both belonged to the needlework guild.

"Welcome, ladies." Pauline was always happy to see Betty and Jean Pettyman, who spent a substantial sum here every month. Before deciding on which project to begin next, they always examined every kit in the place while asking her endless questions.

Bertie exchanged a knowing glance with Pauline, acknowledging that she would be tied up for a while with the sisters. When it came to crafts, they were extremely competitive. Each was determined to produce something more unique, more skillful and more attractive than the other. The problem was that neither had much eye for color or design.

"What can I help you with today?" Pauline asked, including both of them in her question.

To her surprise, Betty glanced down at the floor while Jean, the more outspoken of the two, looked pointedly past Pauline.

"If you don't mind, we'd like Bertie to assist us," she said firmly.

Startled, Pauline felt her smile start to slip. "Of course," she replied, puzzled by Jean's unfriendly manner. "Is there a problem?"

"N-no," Betty almost whispered. "We don't want to take up too much of your time, that's all."

Jean gave an audible sniff. Neither of them had ever married. As the last surviving members of a prominent local family, they lived together in a run-down Georgian mansion. They had never worked at paying jobs, but they belonged to every charitable organization in town and they knew everyone of importance.

"Helping you is the very best use of my time that I could imagine," Pauline said in a reassuring tone.

"That's not what I'm hearing," Jean replied, voice cold. She and Harriet were close friends as well as being the worst gossips and the biggest snobs in the guild. Although Jean wasn't normally as bad as the other woman, neither was someone a local merchant would want for an enemy.

Her sister tugged at her arm. "I think we should just go." Betty was as timid as a field mouse. Unlike Jean, she seemed to abhor controversy.

Jean pulled away from Betty's clawlike grasp. "Not until I buy some black silk. I'm completely out."

Pauline glanced around, relieved to see that no one else had come into the shop. Bertie appeared totally engrossed in a flyer about the Historical Society's annual tour of Victorian homes.

Praying silently for tact, Pauline gripped her hands together tightly in front of her. "Jean, please tell me what's the matter," she prompted gently. "Have I said or done something to offend you?"

To her surprise, Jean shook a bony finger under her nose.

"Harriet told me what you're doing," she said, her wrinkled complexion mottled with color. "It's not me you're offending with your loose ways, girl. It's God himself who should concern you."

Chapter Six

Since Wade couldn't proceed with the repair work until the damp subflooring under the vinyl he'd torn out had a chance to dry, he had time to fix dinner. The last time he'd been stuck reading magazines in a dentist's waiting room, he had learned that number three on the "Top Ten List of Turn-ons for Women" was having a man cook for them.

Wade's culinary skills were rudimentary, but he could follow his mother's recipe for lasagna. After putting it into the oven, he hurried upstairs to shower and change into a gray polo shirt and charcoal Dockers.

As soon as he heard Pauline's car, he popped a loaf of garlic bread into the oven, checked the green salad he'd thrown together earlier and uncorked the bottle of a Washington State wine recommended by the clerk at the specialty shop. The retired sommelier had assured

Wade that the Merlot was the equal of anything California had to offer. Although the man had probably exaggerated in order to promote a local product, Wade thought Pauline might prefer it.

Quickly he stuck his head into the dining room to double-check the table he'd set with maroon place mats he'd found in a side-table drawer. They went nicely with the dark wood and striped wallpaper. He considered turning on the CD player but immediately rejected the idea as cheesy, since he wasn't trying to seduce her.

Not yet. For now, he would settle for showing her just how helpful he could be to have around.

When he heard the back door close, he waited in the kitchen with his arms folded, eager for her reaction. She walked into the kitchen, stopping when she saw him, and inhaled deeply.

She had the look of someone who'd had a tough day at work. Nothing like a home-cooked meal to soften those frown lines.

"What's that wonderful smell?" she almost moaned. "Oh, God, have you been cooking?"

"I fixed dinner," he said proudly. "I hope you're hungry."

She rubbed her forehead with her fingertips. "I've had a real bitch of a day."

"I've got wine," he replied, holding up the bottle. Dealing with customers could be a pain no matter what one was selling, he realized. "I'll pour you a glass."

She hesitated, obviously tempted. "Okay," she relented. "I need to talk to you anyway."

Her tone wasn't encouraging.

"Run upstairs if you need to," he suggested, putting his curiosity on hold. "Everything will keep for a few more minutes."

When she came back down to hover in the dining room doorway, he hoped her freshly brushed hair and renewed lip color were for his benefit. The emerald silk shirt she'd worn home from work with slim black slacks brought out the green in her eyes. She had removed her sandals, and her bare toenails were painted pale pink.

"This looks really nice," she murmured when she saw the table. "You went to a lot of trouble."

Snapping out of his trance, he pulled out her chair. "I enjoyed indulging my domestic side."

"I wouldn't have guessed that you have one," she retorted, sounding more like herself.

Wade poured the wine and handed her one of the crystal glasses he had found in the china cabinet. "There's a lot about me that you don't know," he said, raising his glass in a toast. "Here's to explorations."

She sipped her wine without commenting on his statement. "I like this," she said instead. "Good choice."

Pleased, Wade tasted the Merlot and found that she was right. It was pretty decent. "I'll be right back," he promised, taking the lasagna from the oven before returning with their salads.

"You're making this harder," she muttered as he placed a bowl in front of her.

"We're just sharing a meal," he said as he sat across from her. "You'll feel better if you eat."

She appeared ready to argue, but then she sprinkled

dressing on her salad before handing it to him. For a few moments, they ate in silence. When they were done, he took their bowls to the kitchen.

"Can I help?" she called after him.

"No, thanks," he replied. When he served the lasagna and bread, she breathed in deeply. Her smile, though, seemed rueful.

"Looks and smells divine," she said as he topped up their glasses and she sprinkled grated Parmesan cheese on her food. "Good, too," she mumbled after tasting it.

He thanked her between bites, as hungry as she obviously was.

"Tell me what made today so hard," he coaxed when they both had made serious inroads into their dinners. More bad news about the garage could wait. "Difficult customer?"

She took another healthy sip from her glass. Her hand trembled, and he realized that she was more tense than he'd first thought.

"I warned you about how people here might view this, um, situation," she said, her voice slightly shaky. "First the president of the local needlework guild practically threatened me. And then today one of my best customers confronted me right in the middle of the shop. I was lucky the Canadian tour group had already left or it would have been even worse."

Wade extended his hand, signaling her to slow down. "Wait a minute," he protested, confused. "Start from the beginning. Someone *threatened* you?"

"Well, practically," Pauline replied, tucking a strand of dark-blond hair behind her ear. "She said she would

withdraw her support for me on the city council if I
attract any more negative gossip."

"Good God," he muttered, struggling to accept what
he was hearing. What was next, tar and feathers?

"That was before Dolly left," Pauline continued, "so
I wasn't too concerned."

Like hell, he thought. She had mentioned how much
she wanted that council seat. "So what happened today?"

Briefly she described the sisters' visit while he
chewed and swallowed a bite of the bread.

"What did they want, to brand you with a scarlet *A?*"
he blurted. "The old bats."

"I'm glad you can see the humor in all of this,"
Pauline replied sarcastically before she drank more of
her wine. "One of the worst gossips in town practically
accused me of being a…harlot and you make jokes."

Wade's temper rose. How dare some dried-up old
prunes give Pauline a bad time over something so
trivial. So innocent, at least on her part. "I'm sorry you
had to go through that, but I hope you told her to stuff
it."

"Jean Pettyman and her sister spend a lot of money
at my shop," she explained. "They belong to the needlework guild, and Jean's on the board at the library."
She took a deep breath. "Harriet's husband is on the city
council, and I'm sure he doesn't make a decision
without listening to his wife." Pauline's voice had risen.
Abruptly she stopped, pressing her lips together in a
tight line.

Wade had no patience with people who tried to run
everyone else's lives. "You're not doing anything wrong

and you can't just knuckle under to these judgmental hypocrites." He shoved aside his plate. "Good God, Pauline, what's next, letting them search your bedroom?"

She shook her head. "You don't understand," she said. "I've worked hard to earn people's respect, and now my professional reputation is at risk, all because of—" She broke off abruptly, but he knew what she'd been about to say.

Because of you.

He wanted to protest that giving in to that kind of pressure was just as wrong as the people who were judging her so harshly, but unfortunately for him, her comment invoked a whisper of understanding. Anyone who argued that a professional reputation was immune to petty gossip was just plain naive. He had learned that lesson the hard way.

Unfortunately if he allowed himself to waver in the face of her obvious plan to eject him, he'd be out on the street before he could say the words *platonic relationship*.

The last thing Pauline wanted to do was argue with Wade or force him to move out. He would resent her and she would lose the chance to get to know him better. They wouldn't even be friends.

"I need my regular customers' patronage to get me through the slow season," she explained. "Most of them are older women and they're conservative. If I alienate women like Harriet and Jean, I'll go out of business. It might not seem fair to *you,* but it's *my* reality."

When that old harpy, Jean Pettyman, had confronted

her this afternoon, each scenario Pauline imagined had been worse than the last, until she could easily picture demonstrators with flaming torches picketing her shop.

"Damn," he muttered. "I hate to admit that you have a point, but I know from personal experience that it's a valid one."

If Pauline hadn't been so stunned by his remark, she might have gone over and kissed him out of sheer relief. "Did you say what I thought you did?" she stammered instead.

His smile was rueful, as though he couldn't quite believe it himself. "What we need, my dear, is a solution that will solve both our problems," he said thoughtfully. "A compromise."

"What do you have in mind?" Her hopes, so low a moment ago, rose like a hot-air balloon. Perhaps together they could figure something out so they wouldn't part on a sour note.

She was about to ask what he had meant by his mysterious comment about personal experience, but before she could, he slid back his chair. "If I promise that we'll work this out, would you be able to eat some more pasta?" he asked. "My lasagna is too good to waste, but I could reheat it in the microwave."

Smiling, she handed him her plate. As if by mutual consent, they chatted about other things, including Dolly's last phone call. As soon as they were done, he began clearing the table.

Automatically she scooted back her chair, prepared to help.

"Sit," he instructed her sternly. "I'll bring dessert."

"Don't tell me you had time to make that, too," she exclaimed.

With a plate in each hand, he paused in the kitchen doorway and grinned back at her. "Even I have my limits," he teased. "I bought some spumoni ice cream at the store."

"That sounds perfect," she replied. "Are you sure I can't help with something? I feel a little superfluous just sitting here."

"If that's a serious offer, you could stick around while I clean up." He reappeared with two of her grand-mother's crystal dessert dishes. "I'm afraid I made a real mess of your kitchen."

"Believe me, it was worth it," she reassured him as he served her. "You're spoiling me."

As soon as he sat back down, she dug into her ice cream. As it melted on her tongue, she lifted her brows expectantly.

"Tell me about your family," she suggested. Normally she avoided asking personal questions because they in-variably resulted in the tables being turned on her. Talking about her parents was still painful after all this time, but she couldn't resist the opportunity to learn a little more about this fascinating man who attracted her so strongly.

He seemed to consider her question with care. "My parents retired to Florida a few years back," he said, concentrating his attention on his dessert. He had stuck a wafer cookie into each portion of ice cream. "I hear from them from time to time, but we haven't been close for a couple of years now."

"I'm sorry," Pauline replied after she'd finished

eating. "Do you have any sisters or brothers?" Again she realized that she was opening herself up for turn-about on his part, but his situation saddened her. She knew all too well how painful a family rift could be.

Wade shook his head. "Only child." He touched his napkin to his lips. "You?"

"I have a younger sister down in L.A., but we don't communicate very often, either." What an understate-ment! She and Lily barely kept in touch.

He smiled and glanced up, as if to acknowledge the similarity. "What about your parents? Do they live around here?"

She felt a familiar pang of sadness. "They died in a boating accident while I was away at college." She was proud of herself for keeping her voice steady.

Wade's eyes darkened with shock. "My God," he ex-claimed, covering her hand with his. "I'm sorry to hear that." The warmth of his skin sent a healing balm all through her.

"At least they were doing something they loved." She had reminded herself of that so often it had become a sort of mantra.

"No wonder you don't care to go out on the water." His gaze was intent on her face. "How old were you?"

"Nineteen," she said quietly. Talking about the accident usually made her feel awkward. People never knew what to say, and none of their platitudes made her feel any better. Somehow, though, Wade's interest was comforting in its honesty and its simplicity. He seemed to comprehend the life-changing magnitude of such a loss, even though his parents were still alive.

"What did you do after the accident?" he asked. "It's good that you were able to keep this house."

She shrugged, tearing off a piece of her bread. "There was insurance money, but my sister was only sixteen. I quit school and came home so she wouldn't be shipped off to an out-of-state relative." She could still remember her fierce disappointment, piled on top of the raw grief, but the choice had been clear. Lily had needed her.

"Doing the right thing isn't easy, is it?" he asked. "Even when it's necessary."

She nodded silently, wondering as always if she had been able to see the future, would she have made different choices. Knowing the answer in her heart.

"If you're finished," he said gently, "let me tell you my solution to your earlier dilemma." When she nodded, he folded his hands on the table and leaned toward her.

"I'm nearly finished with the bathroom floor in the apartment above the garage. I'll glue the vinyl down in the morning. Luckily the shower stall is intact, so I can move as soon as I can reset the toilet. The gossipmongers will be silenced, and I can finish the walls later."

Pauline stared as her eyes filled with tears. "You'd do that?" she asked, trying to blink them discreetly away before he noticed. "Even though you've got that signed lease?"

"I told you that I understand, and I do," he confirmed.

Knowing he would still be around was a relief that she

didn't dare analyze. "Shake on it?" She stuck out her hand.

He got to his feet, enclosing her hand in both of his. "I've got a better idea. Stand up for a minute."

When she complied, he leaned toward her. In a purely defensive move, she flattened her free hand on his chest with some hazy idea of warding him off. She could feel his heart beating beneath her palm. The sensation was astonishingly intimate.

When he pressed a kiss to her cheek, the touch of his warm lips kindled a need she had been struggling to ignore since he had first arrived. Before he could pull away, she turned her head. For a moment that seemed to stretch out forever, his silver eyes blazed into hers. How had she ever thought of them as cold?

Chapter Seven

Caught off guard when Pauline moved closer, Wade searched her face. He'd meant only to offer a token of comfort, but her full lips were parted in a silent invitation that he couldn't hope to resist.

He curved his fingers around her delicate jaw, angling her head, and closed his mouth over hers. Pent-up hunger burst into urgent need. Releasing her chin, he gathered her close.

She melted against him as her taste and her throaty moan turned his blood to fire. His body vibrated with desire that had never spiked so quickly or burned as hot from a simple kiss. Finally, reluctantly, he tore his mouth away to drag in a breath that seared his lungs.

She tipped back her head and he nibbled a path up

the smooth skin of her throat. Her scent and taste filled his head, drugged his brain. Burned away his better sense.

He skimmed trembling fingers lightly down her arm. Encircling her wrist that was as delicate as a flower stem, he lifted her hand and pressed an openmouthed kiss to her palm. "Come upstairs with me," he groaned, resisting the mad urge to sink onto the floor, arms wrapped around her legs, and beg. "What do you say?"

She stiffened, but it took his fogged brain a moment to realize that she was pushing him away.

"No!" she moaned, the dreaded word penetrating his desire like a sword. "I'm sorry. No, let me go."

His muscles went rigid, control battling raw need. Coming on so strong to a woman had never been his style, not even this one he wanted so desperately. With a ragged breath, he peeled his arms away and then steadied her when she staggered.

Still as hard as a ball-peen hammer, he tried to read her expression. Her eyes were dark, her satiny lips still inviting.

Wade sucked in another gulp of air, heart knocking, chest heaving as though he'd run a full-out race. "It's okay. It's okay," he chanted both to her and himself as he spread his hands, palms out.

Hell, he was lucky she hadn't grabbed a frying pan in self-defense, the way he'd come at her. As though she were a pork chop and he a wild dog.

"I didn't mean to mislead you," she murmured, twisting her hands together in front of her. "I didn't think I could—"

"Could what?" he demanded, confused, when she stopped abruptly.

"Stir you up like that," she admitted in a rush, her gaze sliding away from his.

Despite his frustration, he had to chuckle as he raked one hand over his head. "Honey, you shot me up like an unmanned rocket," he admitted ruefully. "My brain was completely disengaged, so I'm the one who's sorry." He glanced down at his feet, mildly surprised that his shoes weren't smoking. "I didn't mean to upset you," he added.

The corners of her mouth lifted slightly. "Really? I did all that?" She looked entirely too pleased with herself for his liking.

"Really," he echoed, filing away her reaction for future analysis. "Don't think I can't behave myself," he said quickly so she wouldn't worry about him sneaking into her room at midnight.

Her smug expression faded. "I'm counting on it," she replied softly. "Thank you for the wonderful meal, but I think it's time for me to say good-night."

Wade stared after her as she went up the stairs. If cleaning up the kitchen wasn't enough to work off his frustration, perhaps cutting the vinyl for the bathroom floor would do the trick.

Somehow, though, he doubted that even the old standby—a cold shower—would be enough to banish his sexy landlady from his mind.

After church the next morning, Pauline stopped by the house to grab the keys to the shop that she had forgotten in her haste to get away earlier. She couldn't put off running into Wade indefinitely, but spending a few hours stocking shelves while the shop was closed would give her time to sort out her feelings about the evening before.

His truck was parked in the driveway, but the house was silent. If she was lucky, he'd be working in the garage apartment. If only she never had to face him again, the coward in her wailed silently as she sneaked down the hallway to her room. When she came back out wearing jeans and a sleeveless cotton shirt, she nearly collided with him.

He carried a pile of folded clothing. "Morning," he said briefly.

"Moving already?" she asked, feeling painfully awkward as they backed away from each other.

"The sooner, the better, I figured," he replied, his gaze sliding over her. "You leaving?"

She couldn't very well resent him for doing what she'd asked. If last night had been a one-time thing, brought on by wine and sympathy, she didn't want to know. Not yet, anyway.

She held up the keys to the shop. "I'm going downtown for a while." She swallowed hard, trying not to notice how good he looked in a faded T-shirt that hugged his chest and cutoff jeans that revealed his tanned, muscular legs. He must have showered, because his hair was wet.

Mentally she turned her back before her brain could bring up *that* image.

"Do you have everything you need?" she asked. The garage apartment was only partly furnished, but luckily nothing outside of the bathroom had been damaged by the leak, not even the bed.

"I'll be fine." His silvery eyes revealed nothing of his thoughts.

Perhaps in the light of day, he had come to his senses after all. Or maybe he had a rare condition in which drinking wine brought with it the uncontrollable urge to kiss the next woman he saw.

No, wait. She had made it nearly impossible for him *not* to kiss her.

"I just wanted you to know that you're still welcome to use the kitchen and laundry here at the house," she said, wincing at the prim way she sounded. Awk.

"Thanks." He shifted the pile of clothes. "Well, I'd better let you go." His gaze slid to her mouth, and a shaft of heat nearly singed off her eyelashes, but he didn't pursue it.

How did a woman indicate that she might welcome the pursuit? she wondered as he walked away. How did she find the courage to try?

When she heard the back door shut behind him, she finally went on downstairs to find something to take with her for lunch. In the refrigerator was a square of leftover lasagna covered with plastic. On top was a Post-it note with her name written in his bold scrawl. Right this moment, she wasn't sure which side of his nature attracted her more, sexy stud or talented cook.

After he had finished moving his stuff out of his room, Wade retrieved his CD player, his laptop and a few more clothes from the storage unit that held the balance of his worldly goods. Back at the apartment, he popped in a CD, cranked up some hot sounds and taped the seams on the new bathroom Sheetrock.

Maybe his first impression of Pauline needed tweaking. She was apparently more complex than he'd originally thought, but he never would have guessed her to be unaware of her own attraction. It made him wonder who was responsible for the shadow of uncertainty he'd glimpsed in her eyes before his own pathetic confession.

The part about being an unmanned rocket was especially clever. She had probably been biting the inside of her cheek to keep from howling with laughter. It sure as hell wouldn't be the first time he'd misread a woman's feelings.

He had sure read his ex-wife wrong.

Deliberately he cut off that line of thinking. When he had done everything he could in the bathroom, he organized the rest of the apartment, which consisted of a bedroom and a living-dining-kitchen combo. Compared to his suite at the big house, he was roughing it.

At one point, he heard a car door and looked out in time to see Pauline disappear into the house. He thought about asking if she was interested in getting something to eat, then decided he needed a break.

Masculine company, a burger and cold beer. After he'd cleaned up at the bathroom sink and pulled on a clean but well-worn shirt, he ignored the welcome light pouring from the windows of the house and opted instead for the Crab Pot.

Most nights Steve or some of his buddies could be

found there in search of a pool game. No one would play Wade for real money—not since he had run the table on Brian, the current champ, who after the game had accused Wade of hustling him.

"I got lucky, that's all," Wade had protested. "Doesn't mean I earned your title."

Now they played for beers or quarters, which was fine by Wade. The easy banter—sometimes spiced with a bit of friendly flirting if a woman joined the group—kept him from thinking too much about Pauline and life and the twists that headed a man in a new direction. It would sure as hell beat standing by his apartment window staring at the lights in the big house through the trees and wondering what kind of sap mooned around like that after one mind-blowing kiss.

When he walked into the Crab Pot a few moments later, Steve waved from a corner table.

This was what he needed, Wade thought as he ambled over to the foursome seated there. After the initial round of greetings, he was content to drink the beer someone handed him. After he had ordered a burger, he watched women's softball on the muted television above the bar while Steve and Brian debated the merits of the Seahawks' new quarterback.

Staring up at the screen, Wade finished his burger.

"Got a lot on your mind?" Steve asked when they were the only two at the table. Brian and the other guy, a concrete finisher named George, were playing shuffleboard, and Jose had gone to the head.

"Nah, just stuff," Wade replied, refilling his schooner. "I moved to the garage today."

"Oh, yeah?" Steve's brows lifted. "She throw you out?"

Wade glowered. "Fun-ny." Since when did guys analyze each other's moods, anyway? All he wanted was a beer and some noise. He'd thought about hitting on some female, then dismissed the idea as ridiculous. He'd never seen much point in easy pickups that usually left him with little respect for either the woman or himself. If that wasn't a manly attitude, he didn't much care.

"I've lived in worse places," he added. "Haven't you?"

"Hell, yes," Steve admitted without elaborating. "So why'd you make the switch?"

Wade noticed that George had stopped at another table, where he appeared to be talking earnestly to one of the women seated there.

"Is it something particular that you're fishing for?" Wade asked Steve. "Or are you just trolling to see what you catch?"

"I'm just a curious guy," Steve said. "And Pauline is my friend, so I like to keep tabs. How's she doing?"

Good God, Wade thought. How was a man to get any peace? If he wasn't mooning over her, someone else was asking.

"Do you babysit all your friends like this or just the pretty ones?" he demanded without bothering to hide his sudden irritation.

A muscle twitched under Steve's eye, a sure sign that Wade had hit a nerve. Normally he'd back off, but tonight he was spoiling for something.

"You're way off," Steve said quietly as he raised his schooner and swallowed deeply. "Like I said, she's like my sister."

"You sure?" Wade probed as the other man wiped foam off his mustache. "Why don't I ever see you with a woman, then?"

"I'm picky, same as you, my friend." There was an underlying rod of steel in Steve's voice that Wade hadn't heard before. *Back off,* it said.

He figured it was the same tone that Steve must use on his crew when they needed bossing, but Wade wasn't in the mood to be bossed just now.

"If you say so," he said with a shrug. As he scooped a handful of peanuts from a basket on the table, he gave Steve a smile that said he was full of bull and Wade knew it.

Steve's palms slapped the table as though he was going to shove back his chair. Wade's muscles bunched and his adrenaline surged, but then Steve let out a bark of laughter. His shoulders relaxed and he let go of the table.

"You son of a sea snake," he exclaimed, shaking his head. "You almost had me."

"What do you mean?" Wade asked, unready to let go. Dammit, he just felt like pounding on someone.

"Is there a problem?" The bouncer, a burly giant whose beaded headband and distinctive features marked him as a member of a local tribe, stood over them. His upper arms were huge, his black eyes intense in his wide face.

Wade looked up and so did Steve. "No, Riley," Steve said sheepishly. "No problem."

"None at all," Wade echoed. He'd seen the bouncer in action the other night when he had single-handedly ejected a bull-necked drunk. No way was Wade crazy enough to challenge someone who looked capable of snapping him in half like a turkey wishbone.

The behemoth stared at them both from under beetling black eyebrows, forearms like hams folded across his muscular chest. "Take it outside if things change."

"Sure."

"Okay, yeah." They babbled in agreement like boys confronted by a school principal.

"Phew," Steve said after Riley left. "Feel the floor shake when he walks?"

"That was my heart thudding right up in my throat," Wade drawled in an attempt to make amends for being a jerk.

"I think I wet myself," Steve replied.

Giddy with relief at the near massacre, they both laughed uproariously.

"I saw Riley talking to you." Jose slid a chair next to Steve's. "What did he want?"

"To break us into tiny pieces," Steve replied, winking at Wade.

Jose filled his glass, looking disappointed. "I thought you might get into it."

"Naw, it's all good." Steve reached over to clap Wade on the shoulder just as Brian and George showed up.

"Want another pitcher?" Steve asked, sliding his chair over to make room for them.

Wade glanced at the clock on the far wall beneath a neon beer sign. "Not for me, thanks. I'll see you guys later."

His upbeat mood lasted until he turned into the

driveway back at the house. Stunned, he stared at the front yard, which appeared to have been hit by an out-of-season blizzard. Glowing in the pale light from the moon were yards and yards of toilet paper. Streamers swaddled every branch and shrub, making them look like misshapen mummies. Rolls of it dangled from the willow tree, a crop of bizarre fruit. More of it criss-crossed the grass, turning it into a gigantic crazy quilt.

In the middle of it all was Pauline, fiercely stuffing handfuls of the white stuff into a garbage bag. She couldn't have been working any faster if she were getting paid by the running foot.

Pauline heard the sound of Wade's truck coming down the street. He parked in the driveway, but she didn't bother looking up; she was too busy.

It wasn't fair to be mad at him because someone had TP'd her front yard, but she would bet a day's profits that this act of vandalism was somehow connected to his presence. Life had been simpler before he'd come to town and stirred up everything, including her emotions.

As she went up onto her toes, reaching for an elusive strip of paper dangling just above her fingers, she heard his muffled footsteps on the grass behind her. Quickly she dashed the tears of frustration from her cheeks.

When she turned around, he surprised her with a brief kiss on her lips.

"Mmm, fire and ice," he murmured before plucking the stream of paper from the branch overhead. "What's all this about?"

"Probably just a prank by some kids who got the wrong house," she replied, glad her face was shadowed. It was hard to stay angry when he stood in front of her looking better than any pain in the butt had a right to look. The moonlight turned his spare face and high cheekbones into a sculpture of simple yet elegant planes.

His expression was stern. "Damn shame. Come on, I'll help you." He pulled another bag from the box on the ground and began tearing down the streamers that she hadn't been able to reach. She gathered the ones on the grass until her back started to ache, but as they worked in companionable silence, the knot in her stomach slowly unraveled.

She knew exactly why she was so bothered by the probability that this prank was aimed at her.

Pride. Her parents had always said she had an over-abundance of it—which seemed odd when it was Lily who had loved preening and showing off. Pauline had been the bookworm, the brain, the shy, plain child who hadn't wanted to draw attention to herself.

The one who'd been terrified of failing.

How ironic that she had failed so miserably and so publicly, making one of the biggest, splashiest, most spectacular belly flops this town had seen in a long time.

"The timing of this little prank seems kind of coincidental," Wade commented, breaking into her thoughts as he dragged his full bag over and tied a knot in the top.

"What do you mean?" She felt instantly uncomfortable, as if she were standing outside in her underwear. And not the fancy stuff, either. Plain cotton—with holes.

He shrugged. "I don't suppose those old crones looking to brand your forehead would do this."

"Doesn't seem like their style," she replied, looking around to see if there was any more paper that they had missed.

Silently they dragged the bags past the house as a car drove by. Thank God no one had been by earlier while she'd been cleaning up. It was probably too much to hope that her street had been devoid of traffic before she looked outside.

She lifted the lid from the garbage can and Wade stuffed in both bags. Then he turned away, but not before she heard a muffled chuckle.

She barely resisted the urge to slam down the lid. "What's so funny?" she demanded.

"I was picturing a gang of old ladies, complete with ladder, TPing your yard," he admitted, his smile gleaming in the darkness. It reminded her of the Cheshire cat from *Alice in Wonderland,* who disappeared except for his grin. "Kind of lightens the mood, don't you think?"

It took her a moment to switch gears from the memory of Disney movies with Lily. "Yeah," she agreed. "When you think of it that way, it kind of does."

He moved closer and she could read his intentions. Feeling way too vulnerable, she ducked through the gate and shut it firmly between them.

He stuffed his hands into his pockets. "Chicken," he said softly.

She ignored the jibe. "Thanks for your help," she said stiffly. "I appreciate it."

Feeling like a coward, she went inside without glancing back. Why had she retreated like a scared little girl instead of waiting to see if he would kiss her again?

What had she feared—that he might not?

Locking the door behind her, she walked into the dark, silent kitchen. It was times like this that she missed Dolly's presence the most.

A light went on in the window above the garage, and she could see that he hadn't bothered to close the curtains. She wasn't about to check out the view from upstairs, though, not even if her curiosity kept her awake all night.

Two days later, Pauline began to worry. Not only hadn't she heard from Wade since he'd helped her clean up the front yard, but she was pretty sure that he hadn't moved his truck. She had left a message, but he hadn't called back.

What if he had fallen down the apartment stairs or slipped in the shower and knocked himself unconscious? Telling herself that she was being ridiculous, she finally called Steve. She was braced for some pseudohumorous crack when she explained why she was calling, but to her relief, he took her question seriously.

"I haven't seen him since Sunday night," he replied. "Have you tried calling his cell? Maybe he's got a babe holed up there with him."

"Maybe that's why he didn't answer," she replied, embarrassed.

"Hey, look," Steve said quickly, "I was only kidding. When he left the Crab Pot, he was alone. That's all I know. Do you want me to come over and check on him?"

It was bad enough that Steve knew she was concerned. She could just picture the two men laughing about it together.

"No, thanks," she said emphatically. "I can handle it myself."

"I'm sure he's okay, but let me know if you need me," Steve told her. "Wade's a good guy."

Pauline thanked him and broke the connection. Staring at the receiver, she looked out the kitchen window while she worked up her courage. There was no sign of life from the garage, even though the curtain was still open.

How would she feel if the situation were reversed and she needed help? Would she appreciate his interference or would she resent it? More importantly, what kind of a person would she be if there was a chance that he was in trouble and she ignored him? No one else was going to notice his absence, except Steve, who she had practically ordered to stay away.

Taking a deep breath, she dialed Wade's number. When it went to voice mail again, she ended the call and hit redial. This time the ringing stopped abruptly.

"Hello?" growled a harsh, unrecognizable voice.

Her first thought was that someone had stolen his cell phone.

"Wade, are you okay?" she asked cautiously.

"Yeah, sure." The croaked reply was followed by the sound of coughing.

"Are you sick?" she persisted. "Do you need anything?"

"I'm fine, damn it." There was a loud sneeze, followed by muffled swearing, as if he'd put his hand over the receiver. "Fine," he croaked again.

Before she could say anything more, there was a sharp click, followed by silence.

The ungrateful jerk had hung up on her.

Chapter Eight

Pauline slammed down the receiver, irritated with herself for being concerned about Wade's welfare. She stalked over to the window and looked outside, but she couldn't see any signs of life above the garage. Nibbling on her nail, she paced back and forth for a few minutes before compassion won out over annoyance.

While the canned chicken soup was heating on the stove, she ran upstairs and looked through her medicine cabinet. When she saw her reflection in the mirror, she brushed her hair and slicked on some pale lip gloss in case he wasn't too far gone to notice.

Armed with a tray holding a covered bowl of soup, crackers, orange juice, cold pills, cough medicine and a thermometer, she braved the stairs to his apartment.

When she reached the top, she set down the tray, inhaled deeply to calm her nerves and knocked on his door.

There was no response, so she pounded harder. Finally she pressed her ear to the panel. When she didn't hear anything from inside, she took her key from her pocket and stared down at it indecisively.

Like a sick animal who had holed up in a cave, Wade probably wouldn't appreciate her invading his privacy. Too bad, because she had to know for sure that he was all right. Biting her lip, she unlocked the door and eased it partly open.

"Wade?" she called, knocking again on the panel. "Hello? Wade?"

She could hear him coughing, the rasping hack that made a person feel as though their lungs were being ripped up through their throat. The tortured sound was followed by a harsh, defeated groan.

Pushing the door all the way open, she picked up the tray and carried it inside. She hadn't been here since she and Steve had inspected the damage. On the opposite side of the main room was a short hallway that accessed the bathroom and bedroom. From what she could see, the place wasn't as guy-messy as she had expected.

Except for a couple of dirty glasses by the sink, a rumpled blanket on the old couch and a shirt that had been dropped on the floor, it didn't look bad. The air, though, was stale. After she nudged the door shut with her foot, she set down the tray and opened the window.

"Hello," she called again to warn him of her presence.

"Hey, Pauline," he responded hoarsely from the bedroom.

"I brought you some hot soup and a few other things." She hovered uncertainly by the couch, wondering whether she should leave.

There was no response, but she could hear movement and then he appeared, looking as though he might keel over. His cheeks were flushed and his eyes were bloodshot. His hair was too short to be mussed up, but dark whiskers had sprouted on the lower part of his face. If he weren't clinging weakly to the door frame, he might look deliciously dangerous in his torn T and sweatpants riding low on his hips. She suspected the rustling noise she'd heard before he'd appeared was him yanking them on.

"I don't want you to catch my germs," he said, lurching when he took a step toward her.

"Don't worry about it." She hurried over to help him. "I take supplements, so I'm hardly ever sick."

"Of course you do," he mumbled, swaying.

Afraid he might fall, she circled his lean waist with her arm. A lesser woman might have gotten a lustful jolt from hugging his muscular torso, but she tried to maintain a strictly professional attitude as they moved awkwardly toward the table like the losers in a three-legged race. As soon as she pulled out the chrome chair with her free hand, he collapsed onto it. When he tried to catch his breath, another fit of coughing doubled him over.

"Why didn't you call me?" she scolded, pouring some juice and handing it to him when he straightened. "Have you been to see a doctor?"

He gulped down some juice, nearly choking. "Just a cold," he gasped. "I'm no s-sissy."

"I see you haven't lost your sense of humor," she replied drily. "Have you been able to eat anything?"

"Not much here." He removed the lid from the soup with a hand that trembled and leaned forward to inhale.

His vulnerability sent a wave of compassion through Pauline, followed by painful jabs of guilt. What kind of neighbor was she? Hadn't he helped her clean up that mess in her front yard?

Bending over the bowl, he inhaled deeply. "I owe you…life," he croaked between wheezes as he picked up the spoon. "Anything…yours. Just say…word."

"Not necessary," she assured him, torn between tears and laughter.

"Aah." The heartfelt sigh came after he swallowed some of the broth.

She sat down across from him, watching him carefully as he ate.

"My queen," he mumbled between mouthfuls, making her smile. His sense of humor was one of the things she was learning to love about him.

"Have you been drinking plenty of fluids?" she asked. "Taking your temperature?"

He glanced up wordlessly and rolled his red-rimmed eyes.

"It's important," she persisted, slipping into lecture mode. "You're probably dehydrated, which is why you're so shaky."

He finished the soup while she poured him more

juice. "What are you, a school nurse in your spare time?" he asked, voice noticeably smoother.

What was it about men and illness that turned them into petulant children? "Liquids, rest and aspirin for a cold are just basic health care and common sense," she scolded.

Turning away from her, he began hacking again. As soon as he finished, she poked a spoonful of medicine at him.

"What's this?" Leaning away, he eyed it suspiciously.

"A love potion," she drawled. "Open wide."

His chuckle nearly choked him. When he'd recovered, she again offered the liquid. "Take it."

This time he complied without arguing. Afterward, she could see that he looked exhausted. "Do you need help getting to the bathroom?" she asked.

An expression of profound horror crossed his pale, scruffy face. "I can manage," he choked, his dignity obviously ruffled. To prove his point, he flattened his hands on the table and levered himself upward.

"Just holler if you need me," she said sweetly.

"Yeah, that'll happen," he muttered.

When he staggered down the hall, sweats sagging, and shut the bathroom door firmly behind him, she loaded up the tray and then risked a peek into his bedroom.

Except for the tangled bedding, it was as neat and impersonal as a monk's cell. Quickly she straightened the sheets and plumped up the pillows. He reappeared just as she set a glass of water on the nightstand.

"Take a nap," she ordered as he sat down on the side

of the bed. "And for God's sake, call me if you need anything. Otherwise, I'll be back later to check on you."

"Yeah, thanks." He flipped back the covers she had just straightened. "I mean it. Thank you for everything."

"No problem." She hastened from the room in case he intended removing his sweatpants before he slid into bed. "Get some rest," she called before she took the tray and let herself out.

By the time she reached the house, she was already composing a mental shopping list for the grocery store.

At some time in the night Wade awakened to a cool hand on his brow. From the other room, a light glowed softly.

"Thirsty?" Pauline's voice was soft and low, like an angel's.

He figured he must be hallucinating, but the cold water he sucked through a straw tasted real enough. He meant to drink some more, but when he opened his eyes again, morning light flooded his bedroom. He didn't bother calling for her, because he knew she was gone. Despite the blanket she had tucked under his chin, the place had an empty chill.

When he turned his head, he saw a note stuck to his nightstand next to the pills she had brought over. *Juice in fridge, toast in microwave,* was printed neatly. *Eat!* followed by a smiley face.

After he had staggered to the bathroom, coughing all the way, he downed some more of the nasty liquid and fell back against the pillow. Later he was startled awake by the aroma of more soup. He opened his eyes to see

Pauline frowning down at him. Confused, he glanced at the clock.

It was already the middle of the afternoon.

"You didn't have any breakfast," she scolded, perching on the edge of his bed. "How do you expect to get better without nourishment?"

"You nag just like my mother," he grumbled, pulling himself up to a sitting position so he didn't feel quite so helpless. "Why aren't you at work where you belong?"

She stuck a spoonful of soup in his mouth before he could close it. The warmth slid down his throat like smooth Kentucky bourbon, only better.

"Business was slow, so Bertie's filling in." When she tried to feed him again, he grabbed the spoon, spilling a couple of drops.

"I can do it myself." Lord, he sounded like a cranky four-year-old. "Uh, it's good, though," he added gratefully.

"You must be feeling better," she said with an affronted expression. "You're getting back to your bratty self."

"I'm not bratty," he replied, ignoring the urge to cough. "A little ornery, perhaps."

To his relief, her face lost its pinched look. "I'll second that."

"How long can you stay?" he asked when he'd finished the soup. "I'm getting bored."

"You need rest more than entertainment," she replied, her bossy tone back in spades as she took away the bowl. "I'll stick around for a little while if you promise you'll try to sleep."

"I've been sleeping," he whined, but he lay back down obediently when she reappeared with a thin box, which she opened after she had settled into the chair beside the bed.

"What's that?" he asked when she perched narrow glasses onto her nose and took out a piece of fabric.

God, she looked cute.

She showed him a partially filled-in picture of red tulips in a pot. "This is cross-stitch, the kind of needlework that I sell in my shop," she explained. "Doing it relaxes me. Now close your eyes like you promised."

"I'd relax if you'd talk to me," he countered.

"About what?" Her tone had become guarded.

"Tell me more about your family," he suggested, surprised at how heavy his eyelids felt. "Your sister."

She was quiet for so long that he didn't figure she would comply. "I haven't seen Lily in years," she admitted with a sigh.

"Why not?" Curious, he opened one eye, struggling to remain awake.

She was stitching with green thread. "I guess you could say that we had a disagreement—a pretty big one, I'm afraid."

"What about?" It wasn't his style to pry, but everything about her fascinated him. He wanted to understand her better.

"It's complicated," she murmured, pushing the thread through the fabric.

Smothering a yawn, Wade changed tactics. "But you miss her," he guessed. Even though they had let him down when he'd needed them the most, he still missed his parents.

"Of course," Pauline replied. "Lily's the only family I have left."

He heard the sorrow in her voice.

"Our parents adored her," she continued. "Everyone did."

Wade dozed, missing some of her words. "…any boy she wanted." The last words he thought he heard her say were, *even mine*.

He dreamed that he followed Pauline through the jungle as she searched for her sister. He wanted her to stop and rest, but she refused. "I have to find Lily," she kept saying.

He woke again later when Pauline appeared with more soup and a pint of sherbet. She had a meeting, so she didn't stay.

"Leave a message on my cell if you need anything," she told him after she'd stood over him with more medicine.

"Next time could you come dressed like a nurse?" he asked with a hopeful expression. "A tight white uniform with a real short skirt and one of those cute little hats."

Her lips twitched before she caught herself. "Yeah, that'll happen in your lifetime."

The next morning she brought a few more provisions. She looked tired, so he insisted that he could manage on his own, even though he was desperately lonely. The hours dragged as he tried to fill them with naps and daytime television.

He learned how to faux finish a living room wall, to

bake a whole fish in a pastry shell, to clean almost anything with ordinary kitchen products and what diet supplements would keep him young, virile and thin.

When Pauline didn't show up after work, he wished he hadn't been quite so persuasive. She called, but pride made him insist that he was fine on his own. The next morning, he realized it was true.

He could breathe through his nose without choking, so he swallowed experimentally. His throat was no longer sore and he didn't feel the urge to cough. When he sat up, his head didn't pound, although it spun a little and he saw spots floating by.

Apparently he was going to live, despite Pauline's dire predictions. In truth, she had taken excellent care of him, feeding, medicating, even changing his bed and washing his sheets despite his protests.

The memory of her face when he had asked with a patently innocent expression for her to give him a sponge bath still made him chuckle. Now he scoured a hand over his chin and he realized that he needed a shave. He raised his arm and sniffed. Phew! A hot shower and clean clothes wouldn't be a bad idea, either.

He was halfway to the bathroom when his cell phone rang.

"Did I wake you?" Pauline asked. "Do you want breakfast before I leave for work?"

He scratched his chest through the old T-Shirt. "Thanks, but I'm feeling a lot better," he replied. "I can manage."

She wouldn't relent until he swore not to overdo it.

"I feel guilty enough for taking up so much of your

time," he insisted. "Go to work. Sell thread. I promise to lie around and watch soaps all day if that will make you happy. My mind will turn to mush, but at least I'll be rested."

After they ended the call, he ate some toast. After he had showered and shaved, he began to feel human, so he stuffed his trash in a garbage bag. After he'd gathered up the dirty clothes that he'd refused to let her touch, he headed to the main house.

He would have to think of some way to repay her—flowers, which she obviously loved, or gourmet chocolates. A tourist town like this one must have a candy shop.

While she'd nursed him back to health—albeit without the uniform he'd requested—they'd talked about inconsequential things. The books they liked—biographies and history books for him, thrillers and women's fiction for her. When it came to movies, he leaned toward indie films, while she preferred comedies, but they both avoided horror and violence.

She had loaned him CDs by Sarah McLachlan and a woman named Enya, which he had found relaxing, and he had insisted that she borrow some Whitesnake, Queen and the Stones' Greatest Hits.

Neither had mentioned the passionate kiss he still remembered with a bolt of pure lust. He liked studying her face when she didn't know he was looking. Sometimes her lips moved silently, making him wonder what she was thinking, or she rolled her eyes or scrunched her forehead into furrows. He loved making her laugh, especially when he caught her by surprise. She could be stubborn and overly cautious, but he suspected that a man who gained her trust would never be bored.

He was brewing himself a mug of tea in her kitchen, waiting for the washer to finish, when he heard the sound of a vehicle turning into her driveway. He peered through the window to see Steve climb out of his pickup.

Wade called to him from the back porch before he got to the garage.

"I heard that you were on death's door," Steve said with a big grin as he thudded up the porch steps in his work boots.

"It was just a damned cold, not malaria," Wade replied, leading the way back into the house. "I'm doing laundry. How'd you know I was sick?"

"I ran into Pauline at the drugstore," Steve replied. "She was stocking up on cold medication like she expected a national shortage."

"She's been great," Wade replied. He'd have to reimburse her for all the money she must have spent.

In the kitchen, Steve handed him a couple of DVDs. "Thought you might like to borrow these," he said. "She told me you're getting restless."

"Thanks, man." Wade looked at the titles—a new action flick and a comedy that made him think of Pauline. He didn't have a player at his apartment, but there was one here in the house. Perhaps he could get her to watch it with him. "Nice of you."

Steve shrugged. "No problem. Keep them as long as you like."

"Want something to drink?" Wade offered. "I'm

having tea, but there's soda and beer in the refrigerator." He could restock it when he bought groceries.

"Nah, I'm good." Steve sat down at the kitchen table, sticking his legs out to the side.

The washer buzzed, so Wade transferred the wet clothes to the dryer and then sat in the other chair. "How's work?" he asked, sipping his lemon tea. It wasn't his normal beverage of choice, but it soothed his throat.

"Busy." Steve described the progress he'd made on the house he was building, gesturing enthusiastically as he talked. "We're laying the hardwood floors. You should come by if you feel up to it." He gave Wade directions. "It's a pretty setting with a great view of the water."

"I'll keep it in mind," Wade said. "But first I want to finish painting the Sheetrock in my bathroom."

Steve glanced toward the garage. "How do you like the apartment?"

"If I had a choice, I'd take the upstairs suite here in the house any day," Wade said drily. "The bed's bigger."

"Kind of cramped, are you?" Steve teased.

Wade nodded, but something else was on his mind. If anyone could fill him in, it would be Steve. "What's the deal with Pauline and her sister?"

A muscle jumped in Steve's jaw. "You mean Lily." His voice had cooled. "What did Pauline tell you?"

"Not much, just that they'd had a major disagreement. I thought maybe you could fill in a few blanks," Wade replied, treading carefully. "You and Lily used to date, didn't you?"

"Right again." Steve looked away. "It was a long

time ago," he said as he stared out the window, "before she went chasing after her big break and I married someone else."

Wade waited silently for him to continue.

"Then I got divorced," he muttered, "and I gave up on getting serious with women. It doesn't seem worth the hassle." He looked back at Wade. "Building houses is a lot more fun."

"I hear you," Wade replied affably, not quite ready to drop the subject. "It must have been tough when their folks were killed," he persisted. "You'd think something like that would tighten the bond between whoever's left." Not having any siblings of his own, he thought the apparent estrangement was a damned shame.

"Sometimes things don't work out," Steve replied with a shrug. "That was when Pauline quit college and came back home so that Lily wouldn't have to go live with some relative in Kentucky." He twisted the corner of his mustache between two fingers. "God, I can remember how relieved Lily and I were that she wasn't leaving. First love is so damned intense. I'm surprised that anyone survives it."

Wade began to wonder if the two things were connected, Steve and Lily breaking up and her estrangement with Pauline. "So why did Lily leave after all?"

"You're full of questions," Steve drawled. "I guess you're feeling better." He glanced at his watch and then he pushed back his chair. "Duty calls, my friend."

"Thanks for coming by," Wade told him as they got to their feet. "Maybe I'll check out that house you're building."

"Yeah, do that." Steve hesitated. "Listen, if you want answers, ask Pauline. Once I thought I needed them, but I lost interest in that whole deal a long time ago."

Wade didn't quite buy his denial, but it was obvious that Steve had said all he was going to about the subject.

"Hey, I appreciate the movies," Wade said as he followed Steve to the back door. "I'll get them back to you soon."

"No hurry," Steve said over his shoulder. "Take care."

As Wade closed the back door, the signal on the clothes dryer blared, distracting him. He put his mug in the dishwasher, piled his clothes and the movies into the laundry basket and locked up behind him.

Pauline followed the receptionist down the hall of the old brick courthouse. She hadn't told a soul that she had made the cut for the city council position or that she had another interview after work today.

At lunch she had returned the call responding to her ad for a new tenant, but the woman was a smoker with a small dog. Although she insisted that Bambie didn't bark, Pauline had rules about smoking and pets. Neither of the other two callers had been suitable either, which was discouraging but not yet a crisis. Dolly was still in Portland with her sister and wasn't sure when she'd be back.

Now Pauline tried to compose her thoughts as she was shown into an office containing a long table and several chairs. The room was much less intimidating than the actual council chamber, with its high ceiling and raised dais. Being questioned there before had made her feel as though she were appearing in front of a grand jury.

"Go ahead and sit down," the secretary urged as Pauline hovered in the doorway of the empty room. "Can I get you anything?"

"No, thanks." There was no point in chancing a spill down the front of her light green pantsuit or, worse yet, needing the bathroom at a crucial part of the interview.

"Make yourself comfortable, then." The other woman gave her a sympathetic smile before she left, shutting the door behind her.

Pauline perched on the edge of the lone chair on one side of the long table. She crossed and uncrossed her legs while trying to figure out what to do with her arms. A door she hadn't noticed in the oak-paneled wall opened suddenly, and the four council members filed into the room.

She was going to stand up again, but then she decided against it. She had met them all before, of course, so there were informal greetings all around before they aligned themselves across the table from her like a casual inquisition squad.

"Don't be nervous," advised the president. "We've all reviewed your application, so we just want to get to know you a little better."

For the next few minutes, Pauline endured the small talk meant, no doubt, to put her at ease. Perhaps they were gauging how well she might fit into the group, which had served together for years.

Harriet's husband, Elroy, leaned across the table with a solicitous expression on his narrow face that immediately put Pauline on her guard. She knew that he supported one of the other candidates, an older man who belonged to Elroy's church.

"We were all sorry to hear that dear Mrs. Langley was called out of town for a family emergency," he said with a sympathetic smile that didn't reach his beady little eyes. "It's nice that you don't have to rattle around by yourself in that big house while she's gone."

What a chauvinistic old goat, Pauline thought, and how dare he ignore her professional accomplishments as though they didn't matter!

"I'm managing, thank you," she said sweetly. "Actually my other tenant, Wade Garrett, rents the garage apartment, so I'm sure he'd hear my screams if I needed a big, strong man to save me from something."

A couple of the other council members chuckled, while Elroy's smirk seemed to freeze in place. "Indeed," he said, droopy cheeks flushing.

Let him put that in his pipe, she thought.

"What specific skills and experience would you bring to the table if we were to appoint you?" asked the only woman on the council, an attorney with a local practice.

Pauline mentioned her membership in the Waterfront Business Association. When no one stopped her, she went on to describe the annual street sale she organized in late spring and the winter festival that took place before Christmas. "It was my idea for all the shops to put up outdoor lights," she added. "Some of the displays are really elaborate."

"And quite beautiful," added the attorney with a supportive smile.

After more probing questions that left Pauline feeling wrung out, she worried that she hadn't done as well as she could have.

"Thank you for taking the time to talk to us again," said the council president, getting to his feet to signal the end of the interview. "We'll let you know of our decision."

One by one, the other members shook her hand. Unable to think of anything more to add, Pauline gave them one last smile and left the room. She couldn't help wondering if there was more she could have done to promote herself, but it was out of her hands now.

Maybe Elroy had done her a favor after all, she thought as she walked down the front steps. He'd unwittingly given her the opportunity to mention to any prudes in the room that she wasn't shacked up with the handyman!

When she pulled into her driveway a few minutes later, she was relieved to see Wade's truck parked there. If she didn't talk to someone, she was going to burst.

She was sure that he would keep her comments to himself if she asked. Not only didn't she know a lot of people she felt able to confide in, but her trust in him was growing.

"Do you feel up to sharing a pizza?" she asked after she'd called him on her cell. "I'm buying."

"I could probably manage a couple of slices," he replied. "What time should I come over?"

"I'll order it right now, but it usually takes a half hour for delivery, if that works for you."

"Sounds good." His voice had a husky quality that

always got to her. "Thanks," he added before they hung up.

While she waited for the pizza, she hurried upstairs to change from her work clothes into white shorts and a rust-tone tank top. A date had commented once that the color made her eyes look green, so she added small jade earrings shaped like apples that she had bought during a sightseeing trip to Victoria with Lily.

The two of them had stayed at the Empress Hotel and toured the Butchart Gardens. Despite their estrangement, wearing the earrings still made Pauline feel connected.

She picked up a bottle of green-tea-scented spray cologne, but then she returned it to the counter. This wasn't a date; it was two friends having pizza. Buddies.

No use denying that she was strongly attracted to Wade, but she knew better than to think he felt the same. He was a man and she was handy. When he moved on, she would be wise to make sure the only thing of hers that he took with him was a good reference.

Immediately after the pizza was delivered, there was another knock on the door.

"Come on in," she shouted as she poured sodas over ice—root beer for him and diet cola for her. Not wanting to make a big deal of it, she'd set plates and utensils at the kitchen table.

"Hey," she said when he walked in. "How are you feeling?"

"Bored as hell and ready to get back to work." His face was freshly shaved, his T-shirt was clean and his denim cutoffs hugged his strong thighs.

"Eat first," she teased, pointing to the table. "I think you mentioned a fondness for pepperoni."

"My favorite."

She dished up slices and set their drinks on the table.

"What's new?" he asked after they had both sampled the pizza. "Did something unusual happen today?"

His observation surprised her. "How can you tell?"

"You seem to be revved up about something." He set down the rest of his slice and sat back. "Good or bad?"

"I don't know yet." Briefly she summarized the interview, including Elroy's inappropriate comment.

"What an ass," Wade exclaimed. "That kind of crap has got to be illegal." He shook his head. "Man, you weren't exaggerating about this town, were you?"

She knew what he meant. "Nope. You see now why I was concerned?"

"No kidding. How do you think the interview went?"

"I keep thinking of things I could have said," she admitted. "The other candidate is pretty impressive."

"You're pretty damned impressive, too," he said, surprising her with his vehemence as he raised his glass in a toast. "Here's to the next member of the Crescent Cove city council."

That was the exact moment, she realized later, that she knew she would never again be able to think of Wade as merely a tenant.

Chapter Nine

A midsummer temperature in the eighties was a true scorcher for Crescent Cove. The usual breeze off Admiralty Inlet had deserted the waterfront, turning the old buildings along Harbor Avenue into true brick ovens.

Sweltering despite the ceiling fan circling lazily overhead, Pauline fanned herself with a color chart as she stood at the window. The sun-baked sidewalks were nearly empty. Even the vibrantly colored hanging baskets appeared to droop. Anyone with a choice must have opted for the beach or the water.

At lunchtime, she flipped over the Open sign, locked the front door and donned a floppy sun hat. Walking outside was like stepping onto a griddle, but she carried her sandwich and a bottle of iced tea down to the pier, where the air was slightly cooler. Out on the water where the breeze must still exist, sailboats skimmed the surface like seagulls looking for fish.

While Pauline sat and ate, she watched the green-and-white ferry disgorge a load of vehicles, bicyclists and pedestrians before gobbling a new batch into its maw. With a blast of its horn, the Squamish churned away from the dock on its way back to Whidbey Island.

Nibbling on a cookie, she thought about what Wade had said the night before, that she was *impressive*. Did she dare hope that he was right and that the coveted spot on the council would be hers? If he knew that she used to be known locally as "pitiful Pauline," he might not have been so confident of her victory.

Lord knew she wasn't. If only she had her sister's looks and charm, she would have been a shoo-in, but all she had—all she'd ever had—was brainpower. She prayed that would be enough to win over the council members.

Sighing, she wadded up her trash, dropped it into a nearby container and walked back to the shop. She was surprised that there weren't any customers waiting for her from the ferry, but at least the sun had moved far enough west to leave her front window in the shade.

It was slightly cooler inside but not by much. After she'd splashed water on her hands and face, she took out a sample of Hardanger, an openwork style of embroidery, and began stitching.

When the tide turned and the breeze came up, the sidewalks began to fill. The phone rang several times, but no one called to inform her that she was now a member of city government. At closing time, she counted out the register and wrote up the bank deposit before locking the door behind her.

"Hot day!" said Dao from the shop next door as he wheeled in a sidewalk display of ornately embroidered satin slippers.

"No kidding." Pauline waved before turning to walk down the street in the opposite direction.

When she arrived home, the sight of Wade in shorts and a tank top hosing off his truck in the driveway gave her spirits a welcome lift. Water glistened on the long, lean muscles of his arms and legs. It darkened his clothes. When she got out of her SUV and returned his greeting, she felt like a wilted weed in her wrinkled green slacks and matching blouse. She had worn her hair loose, and it, too, felt limp and heavy against her neck.

"You look frazzled," he said, making her feel even less attractive. Grinning, he flicked the hose in her direction. "If you weren't all dressed up and I weren't a gentleman, I'd help you cool off."

If she had more nerve, she might have plastered herself against him, but it wouldn't lower her temperature. She had better watch her thoughts before she dropped from heat stroke right in the gravel.

She held up her laptop instead. "Don't tempt me. I've got paperwork."

"Your loss," he drawled. "I'm almost done with the truck. And then I'll wash yours if you bring me a beer first."

"Deal." She tossed him her keys before she went inside. "I'll be back out as soon as I change clothes."

The phone rang as she was walking through the dining room. As she listened to the news she had been eagerly awaiting, she remembered the toast Wade had made, predicting success. After she thanked the caller, keeping her voice calm, Pauline replaced the receiver with a hand that shook. Swallowing hard, she went back outside.

Wade looked up with a soapy sponge in his hand. "Hey, lady, where's my beer?" he demanded with an exaggerated frown. "A deal's a deal, and I've already started."

"I'm sorry. I forgot." A buzzing sound filled her ears, making her voice sound faint and hollow, as though she were speaking from inside a barrel. "I just got the council's decision."

"And?" he prompted, straightening. "Are we celebrating?"

Bitter disappointment threatened to engulf her like the overwhelming swell of a rogue tsunami. Her eyes filled with tears and the muscles of her throat tightened so that she couldn't speak. For a moment, all she could do was shake her head as she stared at the ground, struggling for control.

"Oh, honey," he said, dropping the sponge with a wet plop before he came to her with open arms, ignoring the hand she held up to ward him off. "I'm so sorry. They're all fools."

He gathered her close to his solid warmth. Pressing her face against his chest as she clung to him, she felt her control shatter. She began to cry in earnest.

"I thought. I thought…" she gulped between sobs.

"Shush now, it's okay," he murmured into her hair as he rocked her. "I promise, it will be okay. You'll see."

For a moment, she indulged herself, clinging to him as he stroked her back and did his best to comfort her. Sweet as it all felt, his touch and his breath against her neck, there was just no way he could console her for her failure.

She had let herself down.

The slow return of her composure brought with it the realization that she was plastered against him like a barnacle on a ship's hull. Worse, the last thing she wanted to do was let him go.

Ever. Oh, God, what was happening to her?

"I'm sorry." She disentangled herself and turned away to brush the tears from her cheeks. "I didn't mean to break down."

"It meant a lot to you, didn't it?" he said, tucking his hands into his pockets.

How could she explain that she had been battling to regain her self-respect for the last thirteen years? To show the town and its residents that "pitiful Pauline" had been replaced by a confident, competent woman in control of her life. And in no need of *anyone's* pity!

"Yes, it did," she said instead.

"What did they say?" he asked.

She swallowed hard and willed her voice to be steady. "Joyce Bates, one of the council members, was the one who called. She said that while they were impressed with me, blah, blah, blah, they had decided to go with one of the other strong candidates, Marv Hoflind, because he's more experienced."

Wade frowned. "Experienced at what, schmoozing?"

"Mostly at playing golf with Elroy, I think." She

shrugged, knowing she probably sounded like a poor loser but unable to help herself. "Marv also has a hugely successful car dealership out on the highway, so he pays a lot of taxes."

"Marv's Auto World. I've driven past it." Wade stared down at her until she became aware of how awful she must look with her red nose and puffy eyes. Unlike Lily, she had never mastered the art of "crying pretty."

"You can't compete against that kind of political muscle." Wade's expression lightened as he removed his hands from his pockets. "You know what you need?"

"What?" she mumbled.

"A couple of beers, a few laughs and maybe a game of pool to take your mind off this crap." He bent down to grab the hose. "Just give me a couple of minutes to rinse off your car and change my clothes. Then we'll head down to the Crab Pot." As though the idea was a done deal, he turned the water back on and began spraying her SUV.

"I'm sorry, but I don't feel like going anywhere." She backed away from the water. "I'm just going to fix myself something to eat and curl up in front of the TV."

"And brood?" he demanded sharply. "Will it make you feel better to wallow in your disappointment?"

Her disappointment turned to indignation. "I don't *wallow*." The word made her visualize pigs floundering in a mud hole. "And I have a right to be disappointed," she added with a sniff. And she had thought he understood!

"Whatever." He aimed the hose away from her and leaned closer, gaze intent on her face. "Or I could take you to bed," he said, shocking her. "Therapy sex. It's a surefire way to distract you from your troubles."

Therapy sex? She opened and shut her mouth like a fish, words temporarily escaping her.

"Well, which is it?" he asked brashly. "Booze or sex? Either one beats the hell out of sulking alone." He winked. "You decide. But I'm warning you, if you don't make up your mind right now, then I get to choose."

"Uh, I haven't been to the Crab Pot in quite a while," she said faintly. Or had sex either, come to think of it.

She clapped her hand over her mouth, afraid for a second that she'd spoken out loud. His expression hadn't altered, so apparently she'd only thought the revealing comment.

What annoyed her the most wasn't that he'd tricked her into agreeing but that he was probably right. If she stayed home, all she would think about was her disappointment.

"You don't have to do this," she protested, feeling like a charity case.

His gaze slid down her body like a caress. "Honey, it was a win-win situation for me," he drawled with an outrageous leer. "Give me ten minutes, okay?"

His antics brought a reluctant smile to her face as her spirits climbed back out of the cellar. Normally she was pretty good at handling disappointment, but it was nice not to have to handle it alone. "How can I resist such an elegant offer?"

He returned her smile with a flash of white teeth before circling her SUV. "That's my girl."

She stood nibbling her lip, dealing with a whole new slew of emotions, while he finished rinsing the last of the soap in record time. "I'll meet you right here," he said as he turned off the water and rolled up the hose.

"Count on it."

As she watched him bound up the stairs to his apartment, trying to figure out what freight train had hit her, she realized that she needed to do something to her red eyes and streaked face. While she was at it, she might as well change into something more appropriate for a waterfront bar.

Just as soon as she figured out what kind of outfit that might be.

When she came back out a little while later, Wade was waiting in the driveway with his arms folded. He'd changed into jeans and a striped shirt. As soon as he saw Pauline, his expression cleared.

"Wow, you look hot!" he exclaimed, making her blush self-consciously as his approving gaze skimmed over her snug low-cut jeans and the sleeveless pink top that bared a thin slice of her flat midriff.

The excitement that bubbled up inside her had nothing to do with the Crab Pot and everything to do with the man holding out his hand.

"Come on, sweetheart," he said. "Let's go blow off some steam."

Wade helped her into his pickup, trying not to stare at her nicely curved rear in jeans that were tighter than anything else he'd seen her wear.

"I'm sorry for whatever part I had in your being

passed over," he said, feeling a genuine wave of remorse as he drove down the hill toward the water. "I guess I thought you were exaggerating."

For a long moment Pauline remained silent. "I guess I'll never be sure," she said quietly. "But you know, I'm not going to let it matter." Her voice quivered and she swallowed. "This isn't the 1800s," she added. "If I lost because of that—well, I guess I wouldn't want to work with those people anyway."

"Good for you." He reached over to pat her thigh and then left his hand there.

As usual, the parking lot was half-full, but he didn't see Steve's truck. Wade was about to get out of his pickup when Pauline touched his forearm. Her fingers on his skin sent a tingle of reaction through him.

He braced himself to hear that she had changed her mind. But he had no intention of taking her home—not yet.

"Cold feet?" he asked.

When she shook her head, the gold hoops in her ears caught the light. She had worked some magic with her face so that no one would be able to tell that a half hour before she had been crying her eyes out.

"I've decided that you don't have to hide out above the garage if you don't want to stay there," she replied, surprising him. "You can move back into your old room anytime."

"What about your customers?" he asked. "I thought you said some of them had threatened to boycott your shop."

She frowned and he kicked himself for reminding

her. "I'll deal with them." Her voice bristled with determination.

"Good for you," he exclaimed. "Now we've really got something to celebrate."

After they'd gotten out of his truck, he took her hand.

"So you've been here before?" he asked. The slightly seedy tavern didn't seem like her kind of place.

"Not for years," she admitted as they went up the front steps to the battered double doors.

He followed her inside, wondering whether she had come with her girlfriends or a date. The bartender greeted Wade by name, winked at Pauline and asked if they wanted a pitcher.

"That work for you?" Wade asked her.

"Absolutely." She led the way past the pool tables to an empty booth at the edge of the small dance floor.

Wade gave the bartender a thumbs-up and grabbed a couple of menus. Steve had told him once if he'd ever heard the local bands play, he would understand why the Crab Pot didn't have live music. Instead a jukebox played classic rock while a gray-haired couple moved around the floor in perfect unison. After sliding into the booth opposite each other, Wade and Pauline both turned to watch them.

"They look like they've been dancing together for a long time," he said after they had executed a complicated twirl.

"I'm sure they have." Pauline's gaze followed their progress. "Pop Shirley came to the house to fix a broken water pipe one night when I was a kid. I remember that he brought his wife because they were on their way home when Dad called him." She took the menu card Wade handed her. "It's nice to know it can work."

"What can?" Wade asked, glancing up from the list of hot sandwiches.

"Marriage," she replied, sounding wistful. "They still look happy."

Wade glanced at the dance floor again as a ballad started and the woman went into her husband's arms like a ship entering the harbor.

"I'm not the one to ask about happy marriages," Wade said drily, skimming the list of burgers. "What are you going to have?"

Before she answered, a familiar waitress with a helmet of teased red hair approached their booth. A plastic tag pinned to her red-and-black blouse identified her as Char. Expertly she set down a tray with a full pitcher, two schooners and a basket of pretzels.

"Tell me, too, honey," Char exclaimed with a wink at Wade. She filled each glass with beer. "What would you like?"

After they ordered and Char had left, Pauline leaned across the table toward Wade. "Your marriage must have been happy at the beginning."

Her question didn't bother him. Since she had nursed him when he was sick, he felt connected to her in some way. As he took a swig of his beer and considered the subject of his marriage, he realized that since he had moved here he hadn't given Sharon a thought.

Had they been happy? He felt disconnected from that life, as though the divorce had been longer than one year ago.

"I suppose you're right." He cleared his throat and glanced around. The booths on either side of them were empty and the music would keep anyone else from overhearing. In the background was the distinctive snick, snick of pool balls hitting each other. Overlaying it all were the sounds of muffled conversations.

"I thought we were happy." He fiddled with his beer glass. "Turns out I was wrong about her, though."

"I'm sorry," Pauline said softly. "That must have been painful."

"By the time it was officially over, I was past caring," he explained. Except for being plenty pissed off, but he didn't think that was what Pauline meant.

She waited silently. It was one thing he had noticed about her before—that she listened. Women who chattered endlessly drove him nuts.

"I have to take part of the blame for the split," he found himself admitting. "I was a workaholic, putting everything I had into the business. At the time, I thought I was doing it for both of us."

Pauline didn't say a word as she sipped her beer, but her eyes stayed on his face.

"Sharon got bored and then she got lonely," he continued. "At about that time, my partner, John, developed a new interest in taking his boat out by himself. I was too stubborn to ask why." He shook his head at the memory of his own stupidity. "Sap that I was, I worked even harder to take up the slack at the office, which meant I was gone even more."

Pauline's eyes widened with comprehension. "You mean the two of them—"

"Had an affair?" he finished for her. "Oh, yeah. I just wish to hell that had been all."

Before she could ask what he meant, the waitress returned with their meals—fish and chips for Pauline and a steak sandwich for Wade.

"Anything else I can bring you?" she asked after she'd set bottles of ketchup and tartar sauce on the table.

He glanced at Pauline, who shook her head. "No, thanks, Char," he replied. "This will be fine."

"You all enjoy." Snapping her gum, she sashayed away.

While Pauline broke apart a steaming piece of deep-fried cod, Wade took a big bite of his sandwich. Maybe it was time to change the subject. His purpose in bringing her here had been to take her mind off the city council decision, not to depress her with his own tale of woe.

"What did you mean by that last remark?" she asked, dipping a fry into a pool of tartar sauce. "That their affair wasn't all."

While he chewed, he debated silently with himself. "I actually discovered John's other game before I figured out what was going on with Sharon," he said. "One day while he was 'out on the boat,' one of his clients needed some money transferred. John didn't answer his cell, so I had to access the client's account."

"I don't like the sound of this," Pauline murmured. "Then what happened?"

"The client's money wasn't there."

Her forkful of slaw froze halfway to her mouth. "Your partner took it?" she whispered.

"Yep," Wade replied. "That was the beginning of the end." He lifted his glass in a mock salute. "That's when I first learned how unsubstantiated gossip can ruin a person's professional reputation and they can't do a damn thing about it."

No wonder Wade had capitulated so abruptly when she'd insisted that he move out, Pauline realized, studying his face. "So he embezzled the money and you got the blame."

Wade nodded as he calmly chewed and swallowed a mouthful of his sandwich. "Pretty much. John started skimming after he and Sharon first got together. His excuse was that he'd done it for her, but she denied any knowledge of what was going on."

"Didn't he clear you?" she demanded. "You were innocent."

He shrugged. "No one cared. I was there and that was enough, so the business failed."

"That's not fair!" she protested. What he'd been through was a lot worse than her broken engagement, and yet he had moved on.

"No, but it's life. It might have cost me a lot, but it cost John more."

No longer hungry, she pushed aside her cooling meal. "What do you mean?" she asked. "What happened to him?"

"He's serving time for multiple counts, but Sharon wasn't charged at all. Maybe he genuinely loved her and that's why he did it." He glanced down at his plate. "She had a way of making a man want to buy her things, but she always wanted more. Anyway, even though John refused to implicate her, she put the entire blame on to him. After that, the fight went out of him and he pleaded guilty. I was lucky there wasn't enough evidence to charge me, too."

"Is that when you decided to leave California?" she asked after they had both resumed eating.

"There wasn't much left for me there." He wiped his mouth with his napkin. "What the courts didn't take, I sold in an attempt to repay as much as I could."

"What about Sharon? Is she still there?" Maybe that was the real reason Wade had come up here, because running into her would be too difficult after she had helped to ruin him.

"Last I heard, she was in Florida looking for fool number three. And I suspect that she took a good chunk of the money with her."

"Wow." Pauline sipped her beer. Wade's story was a jolting reminder that other people had survived worse things than losing a city council seat.

"Are you done eating?" Wade asked, glancing at her plate.

She pushed it away. "I've had enough." She finished her beer, and Char appeared instantly to top off Pauline's glass before clearing their dishes.

"Want another pitcher?" she asked Wade. "This one's probably warm."

"Maybe later," he told her before returning his attention to Pauline.

"Now that I've told you all about my sordid past, any scandals I should know about in yours?"

"Not really." She was in no mood for another depressing story about people who betrayed those they were supposed to love.

"No secret marriages?" Wade persisted. "How about near misses? A woman as pretty as you must have come close a few times."

"I was engaged," she admitted, flustered by his casual compliment, "but it didn't work out."

He leaned back in his seat, giving every appearance of interest. "What happened?"

She already wished she had kept her big mouth shut.

"I caught him with someone else," she said shortly, "so I broke it off."

His expression sobered. "God, I'm sorry."

"It was a long time ago," she assured him. "It doesn't affect me anymore." Like hell it didn't. She was scared to death of being hurt again.

"Is he still around?" Wade asked. "I could beat him up for you."

"No. He moved away and later on he was killed in a wreck."

"Huh," Wade replied noncommittally. "I hope you were over him by then."

"I was stunned by the news, of course." She hesitated, searching for words. "I wouldn't have wished that kind of fate on anyone. But when I gave back his ring, I knew that I felt more humiliation than actual heartbreak."

"So it wasn't a secret?" Wade probed.

"Word got around." She could remember the glances and whispers as though they'd happened yesterday.

A loud song started playing on the jukebox, giving her an excuse to look away. To her surprise, several couples were on the dance floor.

"Come on," Wade said as he slid from the booth and held out his hand. "Let's dance."

She couldn't very well refuse and leave him standing there. A little action was probably what they both needed to shake off the serious mood that had settled over them.

"Lead the way, Twinkle Toes." She slid her hand into his and allowed him to pull her to her feet.

By the time the raucous number came to an end, Pauline was out of breath. Not only had Wade kept her moving, but his unexpected clowning while they'd danced had made her forget her usual self-consciousness. While not the most talented couple on the floor, they'd probably had the most fun.

As she headed back to their booth, an old ballad began. Catching her wrist, Wade spun her into his arms.

Pauline stared up at him, wide-eyed. "Is this a good idea?" she blurted.

"Let's find out." Pulling her close, he rested his cheek against her hair. This time when the song ended, her feelings were definitely churned up. Part of her wanted to pull back while she still could; the other part would have liked to stay in his arms for the rest of the night.

He leaned down so his breath caressed her cheek and spoke directly into her ear. "Let's get out of here." His voice was rougher than usual, sending a shiver right down to her toes.

She knew what he was asking as well as just how much saying yes would expose her to the kind of risk she had avoided for years. Ever since Carter...and Lily.

Instead of replying, Pauline led Wade from the floor. He stopped at the table long enough to lay down some bills.

"Thanks, you two," Char called out. "Have a good night."

Neither of them spoke on the drive home as slow jazz oozed from the speakers in the cab. She had been a virgin when she'd gotten engaged and a virgin still when she'd broken it off. A few months later, a summer fling had solved that problem, but the experience had been underwhelming, so she hadn't bothered repeating it. All of her dates since then had been casual, just friends hanging out.

She had assumed—incorrectly, as it turned out—that her lack of passion hadn't bothered Carter. Only later had he admitted, hurling the truth like a spear, that his true goal had been the insurance money he'd thought she possessed.

Should she run the risk of Wade's disappointment in her lack of response? Or play it safe and sleep alone? Her choice was made before they reached Mayfield Manor.

He turned off the engine, letting silence fill the cab as they sat in the glow from the light over the garage. Pauline tensed, her palms moist and her mouth dry as she waited for him to make his move.

"Wait for me," he said as he unfastened his seat belt.

Although she was perfectly capable of exiting the pickup without falling on her face, she did as he asked.

After he had assisted her and they stood facing each other, he bent his head and gave her a brief, hard kiss that did little more than tease her.

"Last chance to say no," he warned when she didn't pull away.

She held his gaze, ignoring the out that he offered. With a grin, he curved his arm around her shoulders and led her through the backyard gate.

"Okay?" he asked when they reached the porch.

"A little nervous." Her voice was unnaturally high as she struggled to speak past the lump in her throat. "It's been a while."

"It's like riding a bike." He brushed her lips with his fingertips, making her tremble with longing. "Take me upstairs and I'll show you."

Chapter Ten

"Okay." Pauline's reply was so soft that at first Wade thought he'd heard wrong. Then she lifted her head in silent invitation.

He backed her slowly against the door, bracing his hands on either side of her. He leaned down an inch at a time, tormenting them both, until his mouth hovered over hers.

She made a wordless sound in her throat that nearly shattered his control and then she slid her arms around his neck and tugged, closing the space between them.

As they shared a passionate kiss, he shifted so that he was pressed against the soft, welcoming length of her. At some point, his arms closed around her as he tried to absorb her, to meld with her. He rubbed against her, seeking her heat, and realized that he'd better get her inside.

By the time they reached the kitchen, the last shreds of his conscience were battling his libido. He caught her arm in a loose grip, unable to resist kissing her again. Even though her response was everything he wanted it to be, he reluctantly pulled away before all his blood had a chance to drain from his head and shut down his brain.

"Sweetheart," he murmured, touching his forehead to hers as his pulse raced like a jackhammer, "I may kick myself for asking, but are you sure about this?" What the hell was he trying to do, talk her out of it? Had he lost his mind or was he correct in questioning the extent of her experience?

"What do you mean?" Her eyes were wide, her mouth full and soft.

"It's not too late to stop." Part of him—the part that ached—couldn't believe what he was saying.

"Don't you want me?" she asked in a small voice, attempting to disentangle herself from his embrace.

A fist clenched inside his chest. Not want her?

Not want her?

To his ears, his chuckle sounded as though someone were choking off his air. His hand wasn't quite steady as he tucked a finger under her chin, lifting it gently so he could look into her eyes.

"I'm trying to do the right thing," he admitted grimly. "But don't think for a minute that I don't want to make love to you more than I want my next breath."

He could read her doubt on her face. Apparently someone—maybe her jerk of an unfaithful fiancé—

had dealt her confidence a major blow. Figuring that words wouldn't be enough to convince her otherwise, he took her hand and slid it down his body to the fly of his jeans.

"Not want you?" he repeated hoarsely, stifling a groan as her fingers stroked him through the worn denim. "That's not a diamond cutter in my pocket, sweetheart."

Her eyes gleamed with the sudden awareness of her own power. "How can I be sure without further investigation?" she purred. "Maybe you'd better come with me."

Pauline had no idea where she'd gotten the nerve for that last line. Maybe it was relief that made her almost giddy. All she knew was that the man she wanted was here and there was no doubt, no doubt *at all,* that he wanted her just as much. For once, she was determined to throw aside her usual caution and let impulse take over.

But first she had to ask an embarrassing question. "I didn't exactly plan for this," she said. "I'm not, um, taking anything—"

"It's okay," he said, dropping a kiss on her nose. "I'll protect you, okay?"

"Thank you." With singular purpose, she led him through the shadows to the staircase. Before she could ascend it, he clasped his hands on her waist from behind.

"What's your hurry?" he whispered as he reached around to gently cup her breasts. "We've got all night."

The promise in his voice made her shiver with desire. When his fingers brushed her nipples, she arched her back and rubbed against him intimately. As he caressed her, making her burn with need, she feared that her legs might not carry her all the way up the stairs.

Sliding his hands back to her waist, he nudged her forward before he released her. Her fingers tightened on the banister and she forced herself to move. As though he couldn't bear to let her go, he held her hand until she opened the door to her room and led him inside.

Releasing her, he leaned down and turned on a Tiffany-style lamp by the bed. Its colorful glow altered his appearance, making him look mysterious and slightly menacing as his smile faded.

The change left her breathless, unable to move her feet as she stared up at him with helpless fascination.

"You have no idea how long I've been thinking about this," he whispered hoarsely as he closed the space between them and buried his fingers in her hair.

She expected him to overwhelm her with passion. Instead he wooed her with tenderness. When she would have stripped off her knit top and shrugged out of her jeans, he slowed her hands and took his time with her.

"You stop my breath," he murmured when he uncovered her sheer lace bra. She had a fondness for pretty underwear and now she was glad not to be caught in sturdy white cotton.

Her fingers were clumsy as she fumbled the buttons of his shirt, but finally she freed them and slipped her hands inside. When she stroked the warm, smooth skin of his chest, he tipped back his head and shut his eyes.

"Mmm," he rumbled deep in his throat. "That feels so good."

His approval made her blush, but she didn't stop. And neither did he. She was so caught up in her efforts at peeling off his shirt, finally freeing it from his arms in order to toss it to the chair, that she didn't realize he had removed her bra, as well.

Not until he bent his head.

She had begun to stroke his neck and shoulders when he closed his mouth over the tip of her breast. Her fingers dug into the muscle of his upper arm as sensation shot through her.

She had thought she understood the limits of her ability to feel desire—and passion—but she found out how wrong she had been. Slowly, thoroughly, Wade caressed and coaxed her past those limits, refusing to let her hold back any part of herself, until she lay sprawled on the bed, completely spent, thoroughly loved and every last remaining bit of shyness obliterated.

"You're a machine," she gasped, lacking the energy to move. "I hope you don't expect much more, because you've worn me out." She managed to lift one hand and waggle her fingers. "At this point, I doubt I could raise my legs."

She must be exhausted to blurt out something like that, she realized.

"Don't worry about it," he whispered as he worked his way back up her body. "Just relax."

Much to her surprise, when he rose above her, she found the strength after all, wrapping herself around him as he claimed her. He wrung one last response from her and then she held him as his body shuddered with his own release.

Wade's arms began to tremble. In order not to crush her with his weight, he collapsed onto his side with barely the strength left to gather her close.

"Stay with me," she murmured.

"Gladly." He didn't have the energy to retreat, not yet.

"You're a surprise package," he murmured. "A siren disguised as a prude."

"A surprise to me, too," she whispered, reaching over to switch off the light. "You okay?"

"More than." He settled her head on his shoulder, loving the way she curled against him. It had been a long time since he had been lulled to sleep by the rhythm of someone's even breathing. Someone special.

He felt her body go limp as a cat's and was nearly asleep himself when he heard a noise from downstairs that sounded like the front door opening. Straining his ears, he could hear whispers and a muffled thump.

Still half-convinced he was dreaming, he freed his arm from under Pauline's head.

"Wha?" she murmured.

"Shh. It's okay." He rolled out of bed and groped for his jeans. "Go to sleep. I'll be right back."

A floorboard creaked as though someone was coming upstairs. He struggled to picture the layout of her room. Where was a nice stout brass candlestick when you needed one? Suddenly he recalled the corner fireplace and the set of tools on the hearth. Moving carefully through the shadows, he grabbed the poker.

"What's wrong?" Pauline whispered, sitting up in bed. She held the sheet against her breasts.

Wade waved his hand to silence her, realizing she probably couldn't see him, and then he tightened his grip on the poker and eased open the door.

The would-be burglar froze in the hallway, her white hair glowing in the faint light from the window and her purse over her arm.

"Good evening, Wade," said Dolly Langley. "I was trying to be quiet, but I left a message on Pauline's machine earlier."

Heart thudding, he leaned the poker against the wall and opened the door wider, forgetting that he was only partly dressed. "I guess she didn't get your message."

"I see things have changed since I left," Dolly quipped, head tipped like that of a small, bright-eyed bird.

Pauline came up behind Wade and peered around him. "Hi, Dolly," she said softly. "How's your sister?"

"She's doing better," Dolly replied as though the situation was perfectly ordinary. "I'm sorry to cause such a fuss. I expected to be home earlier, but my plane was delayed."

"You must be exhausted," Pauline replied as Wade shifted awkwardly from one foot to the other. He hadn't been this embarrassed since his mother had found a copy of *Playboy* under his bed.

As if she could read his thoughts, Dolly looked

straight into his face. "Since you're already awake, would you mind bringing my suitcase from the foyer?"

Pauline slipped under the covers, pulling them up to her chin. She had switched on the small bedside lamp when she'd gotten up, so now she left it burning for Wade. When she heard him tell Dolly good-night, she closed her eyes and pretended to be sleeping.

He came quietly into the room. After a moment, she heard clothes rustling, so she opened one eye to see that he was putting on his shirt.

"What are you doing?" she whispered, even though the answer was obvious.

Wade leaned over the bed and gave her a quick kiss. "I figured I had worn out my welcome, so I was going back to my apartment."

"It's not as though Dolly doesn't already know you're here," Pauline argued, trying not to sound needy.

He finished buttoning his shirt as though she hadn't spoken. "I'll see you later."

As soon as he slipped out the door, closing it quietly behind him, she padded to the window. The night was clear and the sky above the trees was full of stars. In a few moments she saw him go out through the gate. When he reached the garage, he looked up at her window. His grin sent a shiver of response right down to her toes. She waved, returning his smile as reaction to everything that had happened this evening threatened to overwhelm her.

As she blinked away tears, he blew her a last kiss and then he disappeared around the side of the garage. She waited until a light went on in his apartment and then she crawled back into bed.

A little of their shared body warmth still lingered. Even though she hugged his pillow like a teddy bear while wondering what, if anything, he was thinking about tonight, she didn't fall asleep for a long time.

When a bizarre dream woke her to a room filled with daylight, she glanced at the clock on her nightstand and bolted from the bed. It would have been nice to fix breakfast for Dolly, but she was an early riser and had probably been up for hours.

After hurrying through her morning routine, Pauline rushed downstairs to find Dolly sitting at the kitchen table with a cup of coffee.

"Good morning," Dolly said brightly. "Would you like some eggs?"

At least she hadn't launched into questions about Wade's presence the night before.

"I'd better settle for toast and coffee," Pauline replied with a twinge of regret. "I overslept, so I'm running a little late." While she popped bread into the toaster and poured coffee, she asked more questions about Dolly's sister.

Dolly refused Pauline's offer of a refill. "She's doing much better, but we were starting to get on each other's nerves and I needed to get ready for my cruise, so here I am."

Pauline buttered her toast and sat down to eat. "I'm sure she appreciates all your help."

Dolly sipped her coffee. "What's new around here?" she asked with an innocent expression.

"I didn't get the city council position," Pauline told her.

Dolly pursed her lips. "I'm sorry. I know how much you wanted it. But you seem to have found something else to fill your spare time."

Chewing her toast, Pauline stared blankly until understanding dawned. She drained her mug and slid back her chair.

"So sorry, but I have to go," she babbled. "Thanks for making the coffee. I'll see you after work."

"Will Wade be here for dinner?" Dolly asked as Pauline grabbed an energy bar and an apple for her lunch.

"Only if you invite him," she retorted. On her way to work, she tried with limited success to close off thoughts of the man who was now more than a tenant so she could focus on the day's schedule.

When Lang showed up during her morning break, Pauline felt as though she were wearing a sign.

"Something is different," Lang said in her usual straightforward manner. "Your smile is bigger."

"Maybe I'm looking forward to a successful day's sales," Pauline bluffed over the rim of her latte.

"Not a business smile," Lang responded firmly. "That is much different."

"How so, oh wise one?" Pauline asked as she started slitting open her mail with a carved teak tool that Lang had given her last Christmas. "And where did you learn this useful knowledge?"

She felt energized this morning, even though she was nervous about seeing Wade again. She refused to think about whether he felt the same.

Lang's black eyes narrowed as she drank her chai tea. "Where I learn skill to read faces is of no consequence," she retorted. "What I want to know is whether smile is put there by the tall man with black hair."

"So you're part analyst and part pit bull." Pauline felt her cheeks grow warm. She hadn't blushed this often in years. "I'm pleading the fifth."

Of course, Lang had no idea what she meant. By the time she'd explained the concept of avoiding self-incrimination, three women had come into the shop. Two of them made a beeline for the round rack that held new kits, but the third hovered near the counter with an expectant expression.

Lang got to her feet. "Very clever, this fifth," she muttered. Apparently sarcasm was one concept that Lang understood very well.

Wade watched a movie with Dolly while he waited restlessly for Pauline. This was the night of her needle-work class. He had resisted the temptation to visit her at work, figuring it might be a little awkward.

Seeing Dolly had been awkward enough, especially when she had winked and given him a thumbs-up.

"It's nice of you to keep me company," Dolly told him now as the end credits scrolled down the screen. "My late husband and I sometimes attended two movies a day before television came along."

"There's nothing like a good Western," Wade replied as he ejected the disc from the DVD player. "Heroes and villains were a lot easier to identify back then."

To his surprise, Dolly reached out and patted his hand. "Some heroes are still pretty easy to spot," she said with a meaningful look.

Before he could think of a reply, he heard Pauline's SUV in the driveway. The feeling of anticipation that surged through him was surprisingly strong. Perhaps he could persuade her to help him find out how well two adults would fit into the single bed in his room.

Dolly covered a yawn with her hand. "Would you mind telling our landlady good-night for me?" she asked, face innocent. "I've got a new book waiting, so I won't be back out of my room tonight."

Wade wasn't sure how he felt about getting the go-ahead from a woman of Dolly's age, but he sure as hell wasn't going to argue. "See you tomorrow," he said as she hurried toward the staircase as though her slip were on fire.

The back door opened just as he strolled into the kitchen with his hands in his pockets. Pauline's tired expression brightened when she saw him.

"What a nice surprise," she exclaimed. "Where's Dolly?"

Straight-faced, he repeated Dolly's message. When he was through, Pauline rolled her eyes.

"You'll have to excuse her," she said. "She's our resident matchmaker, so she can't help herself."

Without commenting, Wade slipped his arms around Pauline's slim waist in order to urge her closer. He could smell her scent, a blend of wildflowers and peach potpourri. "Miss me?" he mumbled into her hair. "I sure missed you."

She tipped back her head, the corners of her eyes crinkling as she smiled up at him. "Uh-huh."

His body's reaction to her nearness was predictable,

so he contented himself with a brief kiss on her soft mouth. "Are you hungry?" He hoped she would say no.

"Not really. I zapped a frozen dinner in the microwave at the shop." She made a face. "Spaghetti and meatballs that tasted like cotton and cardboard."

He resisted the primal urge to lay her down in the middle of the kitchen floor. "Then I have a suggestion that might interest you."

"What's that?" Curiosity made her eyes sparkle. She wasn't the most beautiful woman to ever capture his attention, but there was something in her smile, a hint of vulnerability, that made him want to protect her from being hurt, even by him.

Especially by him. The thought that he might have the power to bring this woman pain was a sobering one.

"Why don't you come over to my apartment and I'll show you the bathroom," he suggested. "I'm very proud of my handiwork."

"Speaking from experience," she whispered with a giggle, "I'd say you have every right to be proud."

In the days that followed, Pauline basked in her newfound idea of being a desirable, sensual woman who had captured the interest of an extremely attractive and attentive male.

Wade kissed her passionately every time he got her alone, including once in the garage when she was looking for the hoe. He left her a funny card on the seat of her SUV and brought over a bouquet of sweet peas for the dining room table. If he had the chance, he would come by her shop with deli sandwiches and cookies. Between customers he would drag her into the office for brief, sweet kisses and naughty suggestions concerning the top of her desk.

Just now when the bell out front interrupted his latest visit, she had to ask him for a rain check.

"It's good on a two-for-one special deal," he drawled, letting her go with obvious reluctance.

Pauline hurried out front, still smiling as she finger-combed her hair.

"Mrs. Jankowitz," she exclaimed, spotting the elderly customer looking at blackwork kits. "How are you today?"

"I'm fine." Mrs. Jankowitz's gaze sharpened, making Pauline feel self-conscious. "My dear, you've never looked healthier," she said. "Are you taking some new tonic?"

At that moment, Wade walked through the door to the back.

Mrs. Jankowitz glanced at him and then back at Pauline. "Ah," she said with a wink. "There's a tonic if I ever saw one."

Pauline was grateful that Wade found time out from working for Steve to mow her yard and help with other chores. She was in the thick of the tourist season at the shop, but after her story hour at the library, she showed him how to research his genealogy. He returned the favor by going with her on her treasure hunts to nearby nurseries.

On her next day off, they drove to Port Angeles to

catch the ferry to Victoria on the southern tip of Vancouver Island. After they had explored the quaint shops full of English china and crystal, they took high tea at the grand old Empress Hotel at the mouth of the harbor.

On another day after work, she treated him to a private picnic on a small, secluded beach tucked below a rocky bluff.

"I haven't been here for years," she told him after they'd eaten. "Lily and I came here a lot." Refusing to let the memories dampen her mood, she took a swallow of her white wine.

Wade set aside his glass. "When are you going to trust me with your secrets?" he asked, tucking a strand of her hair behind her ear.

"I do trust you," she protested automatically. "What makes you think I have secrets?"

"Everyone has them," he replied enigmatically. "No matter. Shall we check out the tide pools?"

It wasn't her secrets that she had trouble entrusting to him, she realized as they walked along the rocky shoreline, it was her heart. Even as she fell, she kept flapping her wings in a vain attempt to save herself.

They spent most of their nights together as she struggled to live in the moment. For once, she was determined not to map out her future. When questions formed on the tip of her tongue—questions about his plans or his feelings—she swallowed them. When her own emotions begged to be voiced, she swallowed them, too. Eventually she managed to convince herself that this time was different.

That Wade was different.

* * *

The summer storm was a wild one, full of rain and wind that reminded Pauline of an earlier night when a certain cottonwood branch had changed her life.

She stood with Wade at the living room window. His arm was firmly anchored around her waist, and her head rested against his shoulder as they watched the flashes of lightning crackle down from the dark purple clouds. Thunder boomed overhead like cannon fire as the storm rolled down the coast.

"It's a good thing that Dolly is staying in Seattle tonight," Pauline said as the rain lessened and the thunder grew fainter. She could still see flashes of lightning on the horizon. "I'd hate for her to miss her cruise because of a rainstorm."

"I would have hated for her to get stuck here with us for the next two weeks," Wade drawled.

She pulled back and lightly slapped his arm. "Behave!"

"That's not what you said earlier," he teased.

While the thunder had crashed overhead and hail had pounded on the windows earlier, their lovemaking had been equally wild. It seemed that every time they came together, Pauline learned something new about her own sensual nature. Her earlier belief that she wasn't a passionate person had now become a very private joke.

"You bring out the best in me," she murmured.

His arm tightened as he kissed her hair. "I want you to believe me when I say that I've never experienced what I share with you."

Hiding her skepticism, she smiled her thanks.

They continued to watch the rain until the wind shifted direction, blurring the window glass.

"Want to watch a movie?" she suggested. "I could make some popcorn."

"I've been fantasizing about that ice cream you brought home from work the other day," he said. "Is there any left?"

His easy use of the word *home* sent a dart of happiness straight to her heart. "The raspberry-fudge? Sorry, but we ate it all," she replied absently. Perhaps they should turn in early tonight so they could lie in each other's arms while they listened to Mother Nature's music drumming against her window.

"That was good stuff," he persisted. "I could feel my arteries snapping shut with every spoonful." His voice rumbled against her ear. "I haven't been able to stop thinking about it."

"And I thought you were thinking about me," she said with a melodramatic sigh.

He swatted her lightly on the hip. "That goes without saying, my sweet. Can't a man satisfy more than one craving at a time?"

"Depends on what you plan to do with the ice cream," she drawled.

His arm tightened. "Now you've sparked my imagination. Where did you buy it?"

She pulled away, laughing up at him. "Hartzell's, down past the marina. They make it on-site. I know they're open late, but you can't be thinking about going down there now." Boldly she rubbed her hip against his in an attempt to distract him.

"Do you mind?" he asked, his perseverance surprising her. "It won't take me but a few minutes."

"Just be careful," she said, her feelings slightly hurt. "Maybe I'll take a shower while you're gone."

"You're making this difficult," he groaned. "What's a man to do?"

Relenting, she reached up to plant a light kiss on his mouth. "Why choose when you can have both?"

"You don't mind?" he asked, searching her face.

Since he put it that way, it was easy for her to be gracious. "Go." She was already making plans for his return. By the time she finished with him, ice cream would be the last thing on his mind.

After another longer kiss, he donned his jacket and baseball cap and dashed into the storm. When he drove past the window, he flashed his headlights. The raindrops caught in their beams, sparkling like diamonds.

Shaking her head, Pauline went upstairs. On a night like this, hot water sounded much more appealing than cold ice cream.

Her shower was delayed for a few minutes by a call from Dolly.

"I just wanted to make sure no more trees have fallen on the house," Dolly said.

"So far, so good," Pauline replied as she laid out a new peach satin teddy. "Enjoy the cruise."

"Would you remind Wade to water my plants?" Dolly asked. "It's so nice of him to volunteer again."

After Pauline promised to convey the message, they said goodbye and ended the call. Pauline stepped into her bathroom, where she stripped off her clothes, clipped up her hair and showered with a new tropical-scented gel from the boutique near her shop. After she had dried herself off, she smoothed lotion on her skin and covered the a teddy with her long robe.

When she heard the front door open, she listened for Wade's voice, but it was the sound of a woman's laughter that lured her to the landing.

What on earth—? She peered over the railing just as Wade glanced up from the foyer.

"Look who I found broken down on the side of the road," he exclaimed with a grin. "How's this for a coincidence?"

The woman clung to Wade's arm while she bent to remove her shoes. When she pushed back her hood and looked up, her face was still stunning despite her wet hair and bedraggled appearance.

Pauline's hands tightened on the banister and she stared in disbelief as the other woman's smile faded.

"Hi, sis," Lily said solemnly. "It's been a while."

Chapter Eleven

"Lily!"

Pauline could hardly believe her eyes when she saw her sister standing in the foyer below. If Lily's face had shown the slightest sign of emotion, Pauline would probably have burst into tears. However, Lily's expression was as calm as if they had seen each other last week.

Pride came to Pauline's rescue as she swallowed hard, reining in her own feelings, and bit the inside of her cheek to keep her tears at bay.

"Hello, Lily," she said coolly, her insides still churning. "Welcome home."

Down in the foyer, Wade's pleased expression changed to one of puzzlement, probably because she wasn't turning cartwheels. Tightening the belt of her robe, she descended the stairs, clinging to the banister for support. For the first time, she noticed a young boy standing by the front door with his hands jammed into his pockets. When she got a good look at him, she nearly lost her footing. The boy's resemblance to her sister was unmistakable.

Lily had a child.

"This is my son, Jordan," Lily said as though she could read Pauline's thoughts. "Honey, this is your Aunt Paulie."

To Pauline's inexperienced eye, the boy appeared to be ten or eleven. The idea that she hadn't known of his existence until now sent a jolt of resentment through her, followed immediately by curiosity. Had the last thirteen years been good ones for Lily?

When Lily touched Jordan's shoulder, he pulled away, but he continued to study Pauline curiously. "You don't look like my mom."

It was the kind of comment that Pauline had heard her entire life before Lily had left. "I know," she said, forcing a smile. "Would you like some cocoa to warm you up?"

He glanced at his mother. "That would be nice," Lily said. "I'm sorry to barge in like this. I was going to call first, but the rental car quit. Thank God Wade stopped to help."

Where had she intended on calling from, the front porch?

"Take off your wet coats." Pauline kept her voice steady with an effort of will. "I'll fix some tea." She didn't care if Lily preferred coffee, but she felt painfully self-conscious in front of Wade, as though she were reading for a part without rehearsal. Remembering how she was dressed under her robe made her want to pull the lapels closed.

He wouldn't look so confused as he hung their coats on the hall tree if she had trusted him with the whole story of what had happened between Lily and herself. Maybe then he would have driven on by and left her rescue to some other poor knight.

"I can heat up some soup, too, if you're hungry," Pauline offered, taking pity on the boy. None of this was his fault.

"Don't go to any trouble," Lily protested without much conviction. She was still slim, in navy blue slacks and a matching knit T, but she'd filled out on top. Either that or she'd had something added.

Jordan whispered something earnestly to her.

"It's okay," Wade told him. "When I was your age, I was hungry all the time."

"Is chicken noodle okay?" Pauline asked.

When he bobbed his head, blue eyes still wary, Lily nudged him with her elbow. "Yes, please, Aunt Paulie," he recited without expression.

"Lily, why don't you show Jordan the powder room? There are towels in the cupboard if you'd like to dry your hair," Pauline suggested, resisting the temptation to ask if her sister remembered its location. "Wade, would you help me in the kitchen, please?"

"I'll be there in a minute," he replied.

Miffed, she left the room. A moment later she heard the front door open and shut.

While the water and soup heated on the stove, she got out mugs and bowls, hoping the mundane tasks would stop her mind from spinning. Concentrating was difficult, but she was grateful for the few minutes alone.

When Wade finally reappeared, fresh raindrops glittered on his dark head.

"I tried to call you," he said, leaning his shoulder against the doorjamb, "but my cell wouldn't work."

"They aren't always reliable here. Not enough towers, I guess." She wanted to throw herself into his arms, seek some kind of reassurance. Instead she set out butter and crackers. "So where exactly did you find them?"

"I passed them on the way to the—" He stopped abruptly, slapping his forehead. "Damn, I forgot the ice cream."

"And you wanted it so badly," she couldn't resist pointing out. Served him right, she thought darkly as she stirred the soup.

"Anyway, there she was with the hood up," he continued, oblivious to Pauline's silent commentary. "I couldn't get the car to start either and then I saw Jordan huddled inside, so I offered them a ride. I had no idea who she was, of course, until she gave me this address."

"I'm sure it was a shock," Pauline agreed. Since he had also stopped to help Dolly, who was no longer young, she couldn't very well suspect his motives.

"I asked if she was your sister, and you know the rest," he added. "I thought you'd be happy, but I sense a lot more going on."

The kettle whistled, so she removed it from the

burner. "It's complicated," was all she could offer as she dished up the soup and filled the mugs.

When she was done, he carried the tray to the dining room while she went to fetch her uninvited guests. When she found them in the parlor, Jordan was stretched out on the love seat, fast asleep, with his head resting in Lily's lap.

"Everything's ready at the dining room table," Pauline said quietly. "Would you rather have a tray?"

"No, that's fine. You and I will have to talk, but not in front of my son," Lily replied with a meaningful look.

Jordan sat up, opening his eyes. They were blue, like his mother's, but his coloring also matched that of someone else, Pauline realized.

Steve Lindstrom.

When Pauline showed her sister and her nephew to adjoining rooms upstairs, Wade followed with the bags he'd retrieved from the car. Until he'd seen the stunned expression on Pauline's face, he'd harbored some fuzzy idea that the sight of her sister would be a wonderful surprise.

After watching the two women sitting across the table from each other, he could tell that he'd been unrealistic. Apparently whatever was wrong between them was more serious than she had let on.

Silently he followed her back downstairs, waiting for some clue as to whether he should return to his apartment for the night.

"Do you want anything?" she asked dully as she began loading dirty dishes onto the tray.

"No, thanks." Abruptly he put his hand on her shoulder. "What's wrong?" he asked softly as he searched her averted face. "I thought you'd be happy."

"I'm just in shock, I guess," she murmured, pulling free so she could finish clearing the table.

"Here, let me take that." He took the full tray to the kitchen, where he began loading the dishwasher.

Pauline bustled around him, putting away the food and wiping off the counters. When there was nothing left to do, he pulled out a chair at the small table and waited expectantly.

"I'm exhausted," she said, standing her ground with her arms folded defensively. She looked rigid enough to shatter if anyone touched her. Other than one moment when she had extended her hand toward Jordan's head and then quickly snatched it back, there had been no hugging, no touching of any kind tonight that he had observed.

"Shall I go?" he asked, determined to not add to her stress.

"No, please don't." Her mouth trembled and her eyes pleaded. "I need you here with me tonight."

It was the first time she had admitted to needing him at all. The force of the simple comment stunned him. He opened his arms, breathing a sigh of relief when she stepped into them and rested her head against his chest.

"You know you can talk to me, don't you?" he asked softly against her hair, realizing with a jolt how much he wanted that from her. No one had put their trust in him for way too long, and he wanted it from Pauline more than anyone.

He had always believed that trust needed to be

earned, but, like respect or love, it only counted if it was freely given. He would just have to be patient.

The tension seemed to go out of her as she lifted her head and pressed a kiss to his jaw. "I know," she said. "Thank you. Shall we go upstairs?"

Despite Wade's reassuring presence and his warmth next to her in the darkness of her room, Pauline didn't sleep well. When the alarm woke her in the morning, she was pressed against his back with her arm tucked around his waist.

Groggily she turned and slapped at the snooze button, intending to leave him with something to think about while she was at work. Before she could slide her hand back under the sheet, the memory of last night's events smacked her with all the finesse of a cold, wet towel.

Ignoring Wade's disappointed murmur, she sat up abruptly and flipped aside the covers. She intended to shower, dress and fix breakfast for everyone before she had to leave for work.

"Where's the fire?" Wade grumbled, patting the empty spot behind him without opening his eyes.

"I have houseguests, remember?" she hissed as she gathered up fresh underwear and hurried to the bathroom. While she waited for the water to heat, she mentally cataloged the available supplies in the kitchen. If she had been thinking, she would have mixed up a coffee cake last night to pop in the oven this morning.

If she had *really* been thinking, she thought as she stepped under the lukewarm spray, she would have warned Wade to keep driving if he happened to see an attractive blonde on the side of the road!

Pauline's hair needed shampooing, but she didn't have time. Muttering words that seldom crossed her lips, she soaped up and rinsed off quickly under the spray that abruptly changed to cold, then back again to warm.

Someone else had turned on the water in the old house.

As she stepped out of the tub, drying off as quickly as she could, Wade appeared in the doorway.

Normally the sight of his gloriously naked body would have at the very least *tempted* her to alter her routine. This morning she barely spared him a glance before yanking on her panties and fumbling with the straps of her bra.

"Good morning," he said, his voice husky with sleep as he bent to cup her breast. "Mmm, nice."

"I'm in a hurry." Ducking around him, she caught a glimpse of her face in the mirror. Why couldn't she be one of those women who woke up looking and feeling as though she'd spent a week being pampered at a spa? She would bet anything that Lily not only looked beautiful, she probably didn't have morning breath, either.

The thought reminded Pauline to grab the bottle of mouthwash. As she swished it around, she caught a glimpse of Wade's disgruntled reflection in the mirror.

"What?" she demanded, yanking a brush through her hair before anchoring it into a loose bun on top of her head.

His sigh was heavy with masculine deprivation. "Nothing," he said as he stepped into the shower and jerked the curtain closed.

Whatever. She had no time to decipher his mood.

Usually she came back upstairs after breakfast to add the final touches, but this morning she applied her makeup before she dressed. Shoving aside the comfortable cotton slacks and camp shirt she had planned to wear to work today, she hauled out a long batik-print skirt she had been saving for a special occasion and pulled off the tags. Carefully, so as not to muss her hair, she worked a coordinating scoop-neck top over her head.

In the adjoining bathroom, the shower quit.

"I'll see you downstairs," she called out as she slipped her feet into wedge-heeled sandals. With a critical glance in the full-length mirror, she plastered on her best hostess smile and slipped out of the room.

The coffee was perking, the bacon being kept warm in the oven and the pancake batter ready to pour when Pauline heard footsteps thumping down the stairs, accompanied by the sound of whispered shushing. Taking a deep breath, she smoothed back her hair and faced the dining room with butterflies flapping in her stomach.

Abruptly the thumping stopped. A moment later, Jordan and his mother appeared in the doorway. Lily's hair spilled past her shoulders like a golden waterfall. She was dressed in snug jeans and a T with a picture of Minnie Mouse on the front. Even without makeup, she was gorgeous.

Compared to her, Pauline felt frumpy and overdressed. "Good morning," she said with a bright, phony smile. "I hope you both slept well."

"Like a log," Lily replied, her expression equally polite.

Jordan remained silent until his mother nudged him. "Morning," he grunted from beneath his Dodgers ball cap. "How big is this place anyway?"

"Pretty big," Pauline replied with a grin that felt more genuine. "Six bedrooms and five baths upstairs."

He didn't reply as he looked around the kitchen.

"I see you've got breakfast started," Lily said. "Can we help? If you've got somewhere to go, we can fend for ourselves."

Pauline glanced at the clock. "I have to leave in forty-five minutes." Instantly she regretted committing herself to that much time, but it was too late to amend it now. "I hope you like pancakes and bacon," she added, pouring circles of batter onto the grill.

"I'm sure Jordan would love some," Lily replied. "Just coffee for me, though, and a piece of fruit if you have any."

"Check the refrigerator." Pauline glanced at Jordan, who still leaned against the door frame looking uncomfortable. "Would you mind setting the dining room table?" she asked him. "Four places, please."

He straightened immediately. "Sure," he said. "Where's the stuff?"

Lily looked up from the refrigerator and frowned.

"In that drawer," Pauline said hastily, pointing. "Place mats to the right and dishes in the cabinet above."

"Hey, kid," Wade said easily as he walked into the kitchen. "Is she putting you to work already?"

"I guess." Jordan returned Wade's grin with a slight smile.

As far as Pauline had noticed, it was the first time since their arrival that Jordan's expression had lightened.

"Good morning, ladies," Wade added with exaggerated politeness, but he didn't come over and bestow on Pauline his customary morning kiss.

"Hi," she replied, as did Lily with a sunny smile.

He fetched a mug from the cupboard. "Coffee ready?" he asked with a casual glance in Pauline's direction.

"Uh-huh." Disappointed, she turned back to the stove.

As he chatted with Lily while she sectioned a grapefruit, he kept handing Jordan more items for the table—the salt and pepper shakers, napkins, butter, sugar and cream.

With one eye on the wall clock and the other on him, Pauline dished up the first round of pancakes and removed the plate of bacon from the oven.

Wade grabbed a mitt from the counter. "Give me those," he said, reaching for both platters.

Before she complied, she leaned forward and pressed a lingering kiss to his mouth just as Lily reappeared in the doorway.

"Oops," Lily exclaimed lightly, "I didn't mean to interrupt. I was looking for the artificial sweetener."

Wade handed the little basket to her before taking the hot food. "No problem."

"Would you grab the juice pitcher, too?" Pauline asked Lily with another pointed glance at the clock in order to keep things moving.

"It smells wonderful," Lily enthused as Wade reappeared. "Maybe I'll have one pancake and a piece of bacon, after all."

"You don't eat much," Wade commented as he followed her from the room.

Impatiently Pauline flipped more pancakes. When they were done, she filled a second plate and took it to the other room.

"Doesn't he have the nicest manners?" Lily exclaimed when he slid back Pauline's chair. "See, Jordan? Real men know how to act in polite company."

He ducked his head, blushing. "Jeez, Mom," he muttered. "Lay off."

Wade leaned over to the boy. "She's got a point, you know," he said. "I learned my manners from my mother."

Lily gave him a grateful smile. "Thank you," she mouthed.

"How long are you planning to visit?" Pauline asked as sweetly as she could manage.

A combination of guilt and uncertainty crossed Lily's face when she glanced at Jordan, who was busy working his way through a pile of food.

"Well, we're not exactly visiting," she said softly.

Both Jordan's and Pauline's forks froze in midair.

"Oh?" Pauline struggled to maintain a tone of mild curiosity, even as her stomach dropped like a stone.

"What do you mean, Mom?" Jordan demanded, his voice rising. "When are we going home?"

Lily reached over and touched his arm. "Remember how I explained that I grew up here in Crescent Cove before I moved to L.A.? I think you'll like it here. Just give it a chance."

"This old house is stupid!" He threw down his fork and shoved his chair back so hard that it fell over as he got to his feet. "I hate it here already!"

"Jordan Richard!" Lily exclaimed, looking shocked.

"I'm going back to California!" he shouted, running from the room.

Pauline and Wade exchanged embarrassed glances as Jordan's feet pounded up the stairs. A door slammed and then the house was silent.

"I'm sorry," Lily said, sliding back her chair, too. Her face was pale. "A very, um, close friend of ours recently passed away and Jordan hasn't really adjusted to the changes. I'd better go—"

"Would it be okay if I went up instead?" Wade interrupted. "Maybe it would help if I talked to him, man-to-man, since I'm a recent transplant, too."

Lily clutched her napkin. "Oh, would you? That would be wonderful. He seems to have really taken to you."

Wade got to his feet. "No problem. It will give you two some time before Pauline has to leave for work." He gave her a meaningful look before leaving the room.

"I'll clean up the kitchen so you won't be late," Lily offered in a subdued voice. "Thank you for breakfast."

They both ignored Jordan's half-empty plate.

Pauline was full of questions, but she began with the most obvious. "Why have you suddenly decided to come back?" She nearly said *come home,* but this hadn't been her sister's home for over a decade. "Was it because of your friend's death?"

What did Lily really want? She looked down at the table, her thick lashes screening her blue eyes and her perfect white teeth worrying her full lower lip.

Sitting across from her, Pauline felt as plain as a brown paper bag on the shelf next to a designer purse. Nothing had changed. Five minutes after the princess walked into a room, Pauline's self-esteem melted away like ice on a griddle. Even Wade hadn't been able to keep his eyes off Lily.

Part of Pauline—the mean and selfish part—wished Lily had gotten fat or her complexion had been baked by the California sunshine instead of lightly tanned and smooth as a latte. Most ordinary women would hate her on sight. Not that Pauline hated her sister— part of her had missed Lily terribly—but why did she have to come home now?

"Contrary to my son's comment, Southern California is really no place to raise a child," Lily explained with a smile that pleaded for understanding. "I want him to grow up here, like I did."

"You're getting a late start," Pauline said drily. "How old is he, ten or eleven?"

To her surprise, Lily looked slightly uncomfortable. Almost immediately, though, the fleeting expression gave way to a proud smile. "Jordan is twelve."

Pauline managed to hide her surprise. No wonder the boy had Steve's coloring. Surely if he'd known he had a son, he would have said something to Pauline.

Wait until he got back and saw what a surprise awaited him. Wade had promised to feed his dogs, so she would have to ask when Steve was due home.

So Lily hadn't left town because of what happened with Carter; she'd left because she was pregnant and didn't want people to find out. After everything Pauline had given up for Lily, she hadn't been willing to confide in her big sister.

It hurt to know that Lily hadn't trusted her. Well, as far as Pauline was concerned, Lily could keep her secrets.

"Relocating must be difficult for both of you," Pauline said noncommittally.

Lily glanced down at her hands, which rested on the table. "I was ready for a change, and children are flexible. Jordan will adjust."

After his outburst, Pauline wondered if his mother was as confident as she sounded.

Raising a child was one of the most important and rewarding things a person could do. It was a challenge that Pauline was eager to accept, but not as a single parent, as Lily had.

Suddenly she realized that if she and Carter hadn't waited to sleep together until after their wedding, she might very well have a son or daughter the same age as her nephew.

"Where do you work?" Lily asked when Pauline glanced at her watch. "I always wondered if you went back to college after I left."

"Nope," Pauline replied. "I started working in a needlework shop downtown. A few years ago I bought it."

Lily's face lit up. "You *own* your own business? That's terrific." Still smiling, she shook her head ruefully. "I never could get the hang of doing those tiny stitches, but you were always so talented that way."

Lily had been too busy going out and having fun to be interested in anything as boring as embroidery, Pauline remembered. She, on the other hand, had had plenty of time to herself when she wasn't cracking the books.

"How did your acting career work out?" Pauline asked, forgetting her resolution to not ask questions. "You must have starred in every play the high school produced."

Lily actually chuckled. "I really thought I was going to set Hollywood on its ear." She was silent for a moment. "Well, I did go to a few auditions, but then everything changed. I ended up going in a different direction."

Stifling her curiosity, Pauline glanced at the clock and grabbed her purse. Since she'd forgotten about packing a lunch, she would have to buy something. "I've got to get going." She was debating whether to say goodbye to Wade when he walked into the kitchen.

He looked surprised to see her. "I figured you'd be gone already."

She didn't know how to answer that, so she didn't reply.

He turned to Lily. "Jordan's looking at some sports magazines. Maybe he and I can play some catch later."

"I'm sure he'd enjoy that," she replied. "Thank you."

Wade looked like a small boy who had been praised by a teacher. The last thing Pauline wanted was to leave him to Lily, but if her shop didn't open on time, a fine would be levied by her very own business association.

Wade must have seen her frown and misinterpreted its cause. "Don't worry," he said with way too much cheer. "I'll take good care of them while you're at work."

That was exactly what concerned her. It certainly wouldn't be the first time that Lily used her charm to poach from her older sister.

Chapter Twelve

"Is it true that your sister's back in town with a child who was fathered by Steve Lindstrom?" asked a young woman who looked vaguely familiar to Pauline. "Lily and I were good friends back in high school." She laughed shrilly, handing Pauline a twenty for her purchase. "I'll never forget how she beat me out for the lead in the senior play, but I think Mr. Fiorito had a thing for her, if you know what I mean."

"Where did you hear all this?" Pauline asked curiously as she rang up one dinky package of floss which she doubted the woman would ever actually use. It was just an excuse to dig for gossip. All morning her customers had come in to browse and to quiz her about Lily.

"My sister-in-law works at the mini-mart in Kingston. She called me after Lily stopped there for gas."

The customer's close-set eyes gleamed avidly as she accepted the stack of change for her thirty-nine-cent purchase. "So is it true about her kid?"

Patience growing thin, Pauline leaned across the counter. "Tell you what," she suggested in a low voice. "Next time you see your good friend Lily, why don't you ask her directly?"

The woman stepped back with an offended sniff. "You don't have to get all high and mighty." Her voice carried easily to the half-dozen other customers in the shop as she shook her finger at Pauline. "I remember how Lily stole your boyfriend, so I'm surprised you're willing to have anything to do with that little tramp."

"It's time for you to leave," Pauline said through clenched teeth. "Next time buy your floss somewhere else."

"Count on it!" The woman spun away and slammed out the door, making the bell dance in her wake.

In the awkward silence that followed her departure, Pauline busied herself rearranging the scissors in the glass display case. She needed a moment to give both her burning cheeks and her temper time to cool off before attempting to deal with anyone else.

"I guess I don't have to ask how your morning's going," murmured one of her regulars, Janice Hunt, as she laid a stack of cross-stitch kits on the counter. "People can be such pills."

"No kidding," Pauline muttered as she rang up Janice's purchases. "News travels fast."

"My husband is friends with that woman's brother, so that's how I heard." She handed over her credit card.

"Well, I hope things work out for both of you. Just ignore everyone else." She signed the receipt and handed it back. "Small minds and all that," she added with a wink.

"Thanks." Pauline gave Janice her credit card. "At least today's sales should be excellent if business keeps up. I've been busy all morning."

Janice accepted the bag with her purchases. "There's always a silver lining."

As Pauline refilled a new display of linen floss, she couldn't help but hope that there would be a silver lining to Lily's homecoming.

Of course Pauline loved her sister, but she wasn't sure whether she could like Lily anymore. They had both changed, so a lot depended on what kind of person Lily had become. Well, Pauline owed it to their parents' memories to give her a chance before jumping to any conclusions. Perhaps she had grown up while she was away.

If she had, it wasn't immediately apparent when Pauline got home. She was exhausted from fending off nosy locals and their prying questions.

The first thing Pauline saw when she came down her street was Lily and Wade engaged in a noisy water fight in the front yard. Belatedly Pauline noticed Jordan, too, but the one who captured her attention was her sister.

As Pauline turned into the driveway, Lily ran barefoot across the grass, shrieking with laughter. Tiny shorts revealed her long, tanned legs. Her damp, skimpy top clung to her curves, and her blond ponytail bobbed like that of a schoolgirl as Wade chased her with a water balloon and Jordan cheered him on.

Compared to her energetic baby sister, Pauline felt as old as dirt and as wilted as dried-out lettuce. It didn't help one bit that Wade wore only cutoffs and no shirt. For once, she felt more like slapping his bare chest than admiring it.

As Lily darted away, he tossed the balloon and nailed her square in the back. She squealed and lost her footing as Jordan whooped. Immediately Wade leaned down, hand outstretched, and said something to her with an earnest expression on his lean face.

Pauline was so busy watching the tableau that she nearly drove into the hedge that bordered one side of the driveway. When she hit the brakes, raising a small cloud of dust, they finally noticed her arrival. Lily waved cheerfully. With water running down his chest in rivulets, evidence of an earlier hit, Wade came trotting over to the SUV.

Pauline had hoped to sneak inside without detection in order to freshen up.

"Hey, babe." Wade leaned through the open window and kissed her. The warmth of his mouth against hers made her feel immensely better. "How was your day?" he asked with a solicitous expression.

"Busy," she replied, mollified. She glanced at Lily, who was helping Jordan pick up the broken balloons. "Word travels fast."

"What do you mean?" Wade asked with a puzzled frown as he hitched up his low-riding cutoffs.

"Everyone wanted to know if Lily had really come back." She wished she hadn't said anything.

His frown disappeared. "Small towns." He shook his head. "I'm sure she'll be pleased to hear that."

Pauline barely stopped herself from rolling her eyes. Men could be so clueless!

"Didn't you work today?" As soon as the words were out, she could have bitten her tongue.

If he thought she sounded like a nagging wife, he gave no sign as he held open her door. "Chuck ran into a problem with the plumbing contractor. He can't call Steve until this evening, so he sent everyone home early."

Pauline slid from behind the wheel, grabbing her purse and her laptop. "I'll change and see about supper," she said wearily. The house was half Lily's, so technically she had every right to stay as long as she wanted.

"No need." Wade took her laptop from her. "Lily mentioned how much Jordan likes pizza, so I'm taking us all out to eat as soon you're ready."

Pauline was tempted to beg off, but they would probably go without her, and that would be worse. Knowing that Wade was only trying to help, she did her best to ignore the little green-eyed gremlin who kept whispering that she was going to lose Wade now that Lily was back. Pauline couldn't allow her own insecurities to undermine their budding relationship or it would be doomed for sure. She had to find the courage to believe in herself. And Wade.

"That sounds like a great idea," she told him, summoning a smile. "I won't be long, I promise."

"Hold on," he said. "I've got to clean up, too." He called out to the others and then he waved them in.

Wade hoped that tonight's outing would help smooth over some of the awkwardness between Pauline and Lily. Ever since he'd brought her and Jordan home, the underlying tension had been thick enough to slice like day-old bread.

Part of him wanted to shake Pauline hard and demand to know whether she had any idea how lucky she was to even have a sibling, someone who shared her blood and her personal history. His own mother had confided that his birth had been much too difficult to endure a second time just to provide his father with another little Garrett.

Looking back, Wade suspected it was the conception and not the delivery that she'd found abhorrent. Too sweaty and awkward for his perfectly groomed, flawlessly poised and thoroughly cold mother to deal with.

Pity Wade's father. No wonder the man strayed occasionally.

When Wade herded their foursome into Bella Pizza and Pasta a little while later, he couldn't tell who seemed more nervous, Lily or Pauline. Conversation on the drive over had been sporadic at best.

"I hope you're all hungry," he said with false heartiness as he held open the heavy front door.

Catching Pauline's gaze, he smiled, wishing he'd thought to mention how pretty she looked with her hair in a clip, her lips shimmery pink and utterly kissable.

After a barely noticeable hesitation, she lifted her chin and led the way inside the popular Italian restaurant like a mother duck with her brood.

A dark-haired girl with huge brown eyes greeted them, flashing twin dimples when she smiled. "We don't have any booths available right now. Would a table do?"

"That's fine," Wade replied. He ended up sitting next to Pauline, facing Lily and Jordan. After the hostess handed out menus and took drink orders, she left.

"That isn't little Gina DeMarco, is it?" Lily whispered loudly. "She looks so grown-up."

"Bella told me she's going to be a senior next year," Pauline replied. "Can you believe it?"

"How is Bella?" Lily asked as she opened her menu.

"Ask her yourself." Pauline smiled at the short, heavyset woman approaching the table. "Here she comes."

"Lily! Lily Mayfield, is that really you?" Bella cried, advancing with open arms.

Lily scooted back her chair and rose to give the older woman a hug. "Still working, I see," Lily said when they broke apart.

Bella slapped a hand to her own generous bosom. "I'm still breathing," she replied. "What else would I do?" She included them all in her grin. "We've got to pay for Gina's college. Maybe then Fredo and I will think about retirement."

Her attention homed in on Jordan. "And who is this young man?" she demanded as he squirmed with embarrassment. "Lily, you have a child?" She leaned down and gave the boy a smacking kiss on the cheek while Wade struggled to swallow his amusement. Jordan looked ready to bolt—or puke—as Lily performed introductions. At his age, Wade would have felt the same.

Bella kissed her fingers. "What a handsome young man. *Magnifico,* Lily!"

Someone shouted Bella's name from the direction of the kitchen. "My lasagna's ready," she said with a sigh. "You enjoy, all of you."

After she hurried away, Lily sat back down, cheeks flushed. Wade would have figured that she would be accustomed to admiring stares, but she appeared nearly as uncomfortable as her son.

When Wade glanced at Pauline, he realized that Bella had barely acknowledged her. He wondered if that was a common occurrence when her sister was around.

Across the table, Jordan had ducked behind his menu. "Can I have the cheeseburger pizza?" he asked Lily. "It's got pickle slices."

"We'll probably order something that everyone is willing to share," she told him. "You like pepperoni, don't you?"

His lower lip jutted out. "I never get anything I want," he grumbled petulantly just as a man wearing a baseball cap and a sweatshirt with the sleeves torn off approached the table. Following him was a woman who was probably his wife.

"I told Renee it was you," the man said loudly to Lily. "When did you get back to town?"

"Hello, Harlan," she said with a faint smile, then leaned past him to nod at Renee. "How have you been?"

"Fine and dandy," he said, chest puffed out. "We've been married going on eight years now."

"Nine!" his wife corrected, sounding annoyed. "So this is your boy? We've got three."

Jordan dived behind his menu again, leaving his mother to deal with the nosy couple.

For the next hour, between deciding what to order and trying to eat, the interruptions continued. Lily attempted to share the spotlight, but Pauline was mostly ignored. Wade was assessed and then dismissed as his idea of a chummy family meal disappeared along with their pizza.

Stoically Pauline continued to nibble on her slice and sip her soda. While Lily was chatting politely to one long-lost acquaintance after another, Wade turned to Pauline more than once with a question or a comment, but she kept her head down and her replies were monosyllabic. Jordan was even worse, picking at the small pizza he'd been allowed to order as though it had become something disgusting.

"I heard you were an actress," persisted one older woman who hovered at Lily's elbow, clutching her purse. "I've never seen you in anything, so you can't be very successful."

"I'm not an actress, I'm a CPA," Lily replied with a touch of pride. "I've done the taxes for people you *have* seen, so if that makes me successful in your estimation, so be it."

"Good for you," Wade said quietly as the woman stalked off.

"A CPA?" Pauline echoed. She couldn't have looked more shocked if Lily had announced that she was a nude lion tamer with the circus. "You must have gone back to school." She sounded accusing.

"I was very fortunate," Lily replied calmly.

Pauline seemed to be struggling with her curiosity. "Arthur Winkle owns a local accounting firm, if you're planning to join one here," she said. "He graduated between my class and yours."

"I wouldn't consider working with that creep." Lily tossed her napkin onto the table next to her plate. "He cornered me in the hall when I was a freshman and felt me up."

Jordan groaned and covered his ears, cheeks flaming.

"You never told me," Pauline exclaimed. "You're just full of secrets, aren't you?"

Wade could see the sudden tension that stiffened Lily's shoulders. "I suppose you're right," she agreed. "I'm sorry." She turned to Wade and he could see the distress on her face. "Thank you so much for bringing us," she said. "I'm getting a bit of a headache, so I think I'll wait outside until everyone is finished."

After she left and Jordan had gone to the restroom, Wade leaned over to Pauline. "Don't you think you were a little hard on her?" he asked. "If there's something you want to know, why don't you just ask her?"

To his surprise, she glared at him through narrowed eyes. "You have no idea of the real story, okay?"

Aware of their audience, he refrained from further comment. If anything, the ride back to the house was even quieter than the trip to the restaurant had been.

"Lily, phone for you!" Pauline shouted up the stairs with her hand pressed over the receiver. When she heard Lily pick up the extension, she hung up quietly.

In the days since their appearance at Bella's, the phone rang frequently for Lily. Even though Pauline was acquainted with many of the callers, they rarely acknowledged her. She was beginning to feel like her sister's answering service.

Most evenings when Pauline got home from working at the shop, Lily and Jordan were already gone, either to dinner at someone's house, a backyard barbecue, a picnic at the beach or out on someone's boat. Pauline was surprised that no one had yet awarded Lily the key to the city or asked her to ride in the upcoming Fourth of July parade down Harbor Avenue.

Lily's old cheerleading uniform was still in the attic if she wanted to wear it.

As Pauline glanced through the mail that her sister had left on the kitchen counter, she emitted a rueful chuckle at the mental image her own twisted sense of humor had painted.

"First time I've seen anyone crack up over bills," Wade drawled from the dining room doorway.

Having thought she was alone, Pauline yelped, thoroughly startled, and dropped the letters she'd been holding.

"Where did you come from?" she demanded sharply.

Wade walked over and scooped up the mail. "I was upstairs," he replied, handing it to her. "Your sister's showerhead needed tightening."

Ignoring the obvious comeback line, Pauline slipped her hands around his neck. "How was your day?" she asked softly, trying to make amends.

He leaned down and gave her an absent peck on the

lips, then stepped back so she had no choice but to either let him go or hang there like an oversize pendant.

"Lily left a note," she said, masking fresh disappointment. "She and Jordan have gone to a party at the Westermeiers' and won't be back until late."

He braced his hip against the edge of the counter and folded his arms. "Is that the same Westermeier who has the antique store across from your shop?"

"The very one." She hadn't meant to let her feelings show, but she had known Karl and Nora for years. It hurt to be excluded, even though part of her acknowledged that Lily had always been the life of any party, while Pauline was usually more of a wallflower. "We've served together on the sidewalk-sale committee, and Karl's on the library board."

"How does he know Lily?" Wade asked, frowning.

Pauline laughed without humor. "Everyone knows Lily."

Wade's eyebrows lifted. "Oh?"

She waved her hand. "No, not like that, but in school she was involved in everything—head cheerleader, the lead in all the plays and a core member of the popular group." She brushed a minuscule crumb from the counter. "Lily and Steve were prom king and queen, too."

His expression cleared. "Ah, yes. You said that they were a couple, but he clammed up tighter than a miser's wallet when I mentioned her."

"I wonder what his reaction will be when he gets back from his trip. It won't take long for him to hear the news."

Wade shifted, curving an arm around Pauline's

shoulder in order to pull her close. "Be patient," he mumbled into her hair. "Right now she's like the new kid in school, but all the interest will die down and things will go back to normal. You'll see."

She wanted to tell him that things as she had known them for the last dozen years—carving out a place for herself in the business community and making a success of her shop—were forever changed now that Lily was home to reclaim the spotlight. Pauline felt like the plain Mayfield sister again.

Instead she melted against him, grateful for his understanding as she inhaled his scent. When his arms tightened and his breath caught, hunger sizzled through her and she pressed closer, pleased by his immediate response. With a child now in residence, they usually tried to be discreet, but the next few hours were theirs.

Boldly arching her back so that her hips ground against him, she traced a line down his cheek with her finger.

"Come upstairs," she suggested, voice laden with promise. "I've missed you."

He leaned down to press kisses along the side of her throat. His warm breath and warmer tongue caressed the sensitive skin there, making her shiver with longing as he nibbled a path to her mouth. She tunneled both hands under the hem of his shirt in order to stroke the satiny skin of his back.

He groaned deep in his throat and angled his mouth, taking the kiss deeper. When they finally broke apart, gasping for air, his eyes were heavy-lidded and their normally cool silver had turned hot and smoky.

Before she could guess his intentions, his hands bit into her waist and he lifted her to the counter facing him. He pushed up her skirt and stepped between her parted thighs. Hands on her bare knees, he slid her forward so that she was pressed against him intimately.

"Hold on to my shoulders," he whispered harshly as he rubbed the hard ridge of his erection against the thin silk veiling her moist heat.

Sensation rippled through her. Tightening her grip, she squirmed closer. Her world narrowed, fixating on Wade and the desire building between them.

The sound of tires on gravel outside was an unwelcome intrusion as she hovered on the brink of satisfaction.

"Wait," she gasped, torn between frustration and oblivion. "Someone's here."

Face flushed, Wade turned his head to look out the side window.

"Aw, hell," he groaned, touching his forehead to hers. "They're home early."

Carefully he retreated, lifting Pauline down from her perch as though she were no heavier than a bag of sugar. She felt as though her shaky legs would buckle beneath her as she straightened her clothing and smoothed her hair.

"Ready for company?" she asked Wade, who was busy adjusting his jeans.

"Sure thing." His voice was tight as he looked down at himself with a rueful expression. "That worked like a bucket of cold water."

Pauline couldn't help herself. His dry tone made her giggle. Apparently the humor was infectious, because when Lily and Jordan walked through the back door, they were both laughing uproariously.

"What's the joke?" Lily asked. She looked a little frazzled and Jordan's face was unusually pale.

"Nothing." Pauline wiped her eyes, sobering instantly. "Did your party break up early?"

"You okay, buddy?" Wade asked Jordan as he straggled into the kitchen, thin shoulders drooping.

"He ate too much junk." Gently Lily smoothed back his hair. "He got sick, so here we are."

"I puked on their patio," Jordan elaborated with a touch of boyish pride. "It was gross."

"There's some nausea medication in my medicine cabinet," Pauline offered. "It probably has a children's dose on the bottle."

"Thanks," Lily replied, glancing from her to Wade and back. "I hope we didn't interrupt anything."

Wade shook his head while Pauline's cheeks flamed. "No problem," he said.

Pauline felt like climbing the dining room draperies. "Were you going to show me those paint samples over at your apartment?" she asked pointedly.

"Paint samples?" he repeated with a blank expression.

She wanted to kick him. "For the bedroom?"

If he didn't get her meaning, Lily apparently did. "I need to get Jordan into bed."

"I think we've got crackers, but I could run to the store for some ginger ale," Wade offered. "That's what I always had when I got sick."

Lily's smile lit up her face. "Oh, would you? That sounds like a great idea, but I didn't want to leave him."

"Sure thing." Wade reached out to squeeze Jordan's shoulder. "We'll get you fixed up," he said, digging his keys from his pocket.

Belatedly he turned to Pauline as though he'd forgotten all about her. "I'll be back in a little while," he said. "Is there anything else we need?"

She was wildly tempted to suggest that he bring her back something operated with a battery. Swallowing her frustration, she said sweetly, "No, that's okay. All I want is for our boy to feel better."

When he left, she followed him to the laundry room.

"Later," he said with a cocky grin.

She wanted to bean him with the empty bucket. Instead she grabbed it and a couple of plastic bags. "Just in case," she told Lily as she led her son upstairs.

Restlessly Pauline wandered back into the tidy kitchen, looking for a distraction until Wade returned. Through the window her garden beckoned, and she was definitely in the mood to rip out some weeds.

When she heard Wade's return, she turned around, but he must not have seen her kneeling by the petunias as he hurried up the back steps. The minutes ticked by while she waited for him to reappear.

As she deadheaded a clump of pansies, she tortured herself by picturing him wishing he had met Lily first. It was obvious that he liked Jordan, so having a ready-made stepson wouldn't be a deterrent, especially since Wade and Steve were already buddies. How cozy!

Pauline sat back on her heels and frowned at the hollyhock spikes in front of the fence. If Wade was in danger of falling under Lily's spell, there was nothing *she* could do to stop him.

Or to prevent her own heart from being broken yet again.

Chapter Thirteen

The minutes ticked by as Pauline finished the weeding and still Wade didn't reappear. What could he be doing?

Telling herself she was being ridiculous, she stowed her hand tools and gloves in the garage, tossed the weeds onto the compost heap and stared indecisively at the back of the house. Finally she went quietly up the steps to the porch.

Heart pounding, she eased open the door and sneaked into her own house like a cat burglar. Guilt stabbed her for mistrusting Wade, who had done nothing to earn such lack of faith. But she had to *know*. Experience had taught her that as painful as betrayal itself was the feeling of being played for a fool by people she trusted the most.

She hadn't suspected a thing before she had found

her sister in her fiancé's arms. *"Fool me once, shame on you. Fool me twice…"* she recited silently as she crossed the kitchen.

When she heard Wade's voice through the doorway, she froze.

"It's going to be okay," he said. "Trust me. It will all work out."

Pauline began to tremble all over. Her stomach knotted and her head filled with a dull roar, but she could still hear what was being said.

"I don't know what I'd do without you," Lily replied, her voice muffled.

Heart pounding, Pauline went through the carpeted dining room. When she reached the foyer, she saw that her biggest fear—her worst nightmare—was replaying before her eyes.

Wade stood in the open parlor doorway with his arms around her sister.

Unable to breathe, Pauline blinked hard to clear her vision. She must have made a choked sound of dismay, because they both looked up. Immediately Lily sprang away from him.

"Paulie, it's not what you think!" she exclaimed. "Wade was only—"

"Comforting you?" Pauline finished acidly as she sauntered across the foyer. "I'll have to admit that you work fast, sister dear. You must have refined your tactics."

"Pauline, what the hell are you saying?" Wade demanded, face red. "There's no need to talk like that."

"No need?" Pauline echoed shrilly. "Don't tell me what I *need!*"

It was her own fault for tuning out her instincts. Ever since Lily had shown up, Pauline could feel Wade drifting away from her. What had made her think she could hold on to someone as attractive, smart and funny as he when she hadn't been able to hang on to Carter Black, who had sworn on bended knee that he wanted to spend his life with her?

"I've seen the way you looked at Lily when you didn't think I noticed," she cried.

"Dammit, don't say something you'll regret later," Wade replied, his scowl furrowing his forehead.

His calmness only escalated her own temper. "Maybe you'd like me to move out so the three of you can play house," she baited. "Admit it. That's what you really want now that you've seen Lily, isn't it? *Isn't it?*"

His eyes actually widened for a moment, but then they narrowed into icy silver slits that made her shiver as he came close enough to stand over her.

"So you don't want an explanation?" For some reason the very softness of his voice was more intimidating than if he'd shouted at her.

For once, she refused to be cowed or conned or played for a fool! "I don't need one!" Her voice trembled, infuriating her further. "I've got a mirror, so I understand all too well what's going on. Just don't stand there and lie to me!"

For a long, tense moment he didn't move, although a muscle jumped in his cheek. "Is that why you've been cold to Lily, because you're so jealous that you can't stand it?"

"I have plenty of reasons to be wary of her, believe me! You don't know—"

"Apparently *you* don't know!" He jabbed a finger at her. "For God's sake, maybe you should talk to a professional before this sick fantasy of yours takes over your life!"

"How can you defend her?" Somehow the heartbreak and the fury got all mixed up together, making her desperate to lash out. Without thinking, she lifted her hand.

Wade didn't move, but Lily's sharp gasp was like a dash of cold water. Horrified, Pauline stared at her own raised arm as though it belonged to someone else.

Stunned by what she had nearly done, she was instantly contrite. Her anger evaporated, replaced by regret so painful that it nearly doubled her over. She hadn't been tempted to strike anyone since she and Lily were children. Pauline wanted to tell him that she hadn't meant it—any of it—but her mind had gone blank.

Wade turned to Lily, who stood with her hands clenched together as though she were praying. "I'll talk to you later," he said, his voice flat.

"Okay." She sounded breathless.

Without a word to Pauline, he turned and walked stiffly away.

"Oh, Paulie," Lily wailed softly. "What have you done?"

Trust Lily to turn things around so that *she* was blameless, just like last time. Pauline brushed past her and hurried upstairs to the sanctuary of her room. Shutting the door behind her, she stifled her sobs as she slid down the wall. When she reached the floor, the pain washed over her and she cried until she had no more tears.

* * *

Pauline dragged herself home the next evening from what seemed like the longest day she'd ever spent at the shop. The driveway was empty, so Wade must still be out. She owed him an apology, but she would rather bungee jump off the Space Needle than face him.

When she walked into the house, she was surprised to see Lily seated at the kitchen table with a glass of iced tea in front of her.

"How's Jordan?" Pauline asked brusquely.

"Completely recovered," Lily replied. "He's visiting a boy he met last week."

Pauline didn't bother to ask the boy's name, even though she probably knew the family. She opened the refrigerator and grabbed a soda to take with her upstairs.

"If you've got a minute, you and I need to talk," Lily said before Pauline could leave.

"I don't have anything to say," Pauline replied stubbornly as she opened her soda.

"Wade's moved out," Lily said baldly. "He's going to stay at Steve's."

Pauline felt as though she had been punched in the stomach. "That'll make it awkward for you to visit him," she sneered as she struggled to recover from the news. "Tell me, did you ever tell Steve about Jordan?"

Lily ignored her question. "I understand why you reacted like you did yesterday," she said. "Paulie, kissing Carter that day wasn't my idea, and I swear that nothing is going on between Wade and me."

Pauline had watched long enough to see her sister attempting to get away from Carter, but then Lily had left town before Pauline had had the opportunity to tell her that.

"I never blamed you for Carter," Pauline said. "You were only eighteen and you couldn't help encouraging him. But he was an adult and he should have known better."

Lily's tears spilled down her cheeks and her lips trembled. "Thank you, Paulie," she said hoarsely. "Carter was a jerk who didn't deserve you."

"You shouldn't speak ill of the dead," Pauline muttered.

Lily seemed to freeze. "Dead? Carter? What do you mean?"

Next to Wade, he was the last person Pauline wanted to discuss. "I didn't kill him, if that's what you're thinking," she retorted.

Lily's mouth dropped open.

"I heard indirectly from his mother a few years ago that after his marriage to a Seattle attorney failed, he moved to San Diego. He was killed in an accident."

"I had no idea." Lily seemed dazed by the news.

Had Pauline been wrong in thinking her sister had been blameless? "You look like you just lost your best friend," she drawled.

Immediately Lily's pale cheeks turned pink. "I swear that I never saw or heard from Carter after that day. I hope you believe me."

Pauline shrugged as though it didn't really matter. "Whatever. It was the way you left that hurt me the most," she added. "I needed your support, but you weren't here."

"Because I was ashamed," Lily said. "You broke your engagement because of me."

"Because of Carter," Pauline corrected her.

Lily nodded. "About Wade—" she began.

"That's different. I know what I saw." Pauline drank some of her soda and then she turned to leave the room.

"Wait," Lily insisted. "Even if I *wanted* to steal Wade—which I swear on my son's life *never* crossed my mind—I've seen the way the man looks at you, big sister. He's got it bad."

"Do you think so?" The question slipped out before Pauline could prevent it. She wanted so badly to believe Lily, but the practical, life-isn't-a-romance-novel side of her wouldn't allow her to buy it.

"Then what—?" she couldn't help but start to ask before biting her lip in frustration. She and Lily weren't soul sisters discussing boys, not anymore.

Tears flooded Lily's blue eyes. "Jordan had just blasted me about how unfair I was to make him stay here," she explained, wiping her cheeks with a napkin. "He said he h-hates me." Fresh tears promptly welled up again in her eyes. "I know kids say that, but not Jordan, not before now. Naturally it shook me up."

She looked so sincere that Pauline had to remind herself of Lily's acting experience.

"Wade's a nice guy," Lily added. "He was comforting me. I swear that was *all* there was to it."

Pauline didn't know what to think. "Lily—"

"If you can't believe me, then trust Wade," Lily interrupted. When Pauline didn't reply, her eyes narrowed. "You do trust him, don't you, Paulie?"

"Trust has never come easy for me, not after what

happened with Carter," Pauline replied honestly. "You don't know what it was like around here."

Lily glanced at her hands. "Like you said, I was only eighteen. I—I couldn't face you."

This wasn't getting them anywhere. "I'm going upstairs," Pauline told her.

"You said that trust is hard for you," Lily argued. "If you can't trust me—or Wade—then trust your own instincts. You know Wade's a good guy. Just think about it, that's all I ask."

Reluctantly Pauline began to wonder. Could what she'd heard him say have been words of sympathy and not passion? She could imagine him offering comfort when he saw that Lily was upset; it was part of his nature.

"Oh, God," she groaned, dropping into the other chair and shielding her eyes with her hand. "I was horrible to him. What have I done?"

"He knows about what happened before, doesn't he?" Lily asked. "If you explain—"

"I didn't tell him everything," Pauline admitted. "I was too embarrassed."

"I'm sorry," Lily said softly. She reached across the table to pat Pauline's hand. "Do you want me to talk to him?"

"No!" Pauline retorted. "But thanks for offering," she amended as she got up from the table. "Anyway, it's too late." How could she explain to someone who was used to men falling all over her that Wade's feelings just weren't strong enough to survive Pauline's lack of trust?

* * *

"It's nice of you to let me crash here for a little while," Wade said as he lowered himself into a deck chair on Steve's patio overlooking the water.

Steve handed him a cold brew. "No problem, man. I was sorry to hear that you needed to split. I thought you and Pauline were getting along pretty good." He sprawled onto a lounge chair and took a long pull of his own beer.

"We were until her sister showed up," Wade replied. "Not that it was Lily's fault." He glanced at Steve, who had sat up abruptly.

"Lily's back?" he demanded, his normally placid expression turning hard. "When?" He took another deep swig, nearly emptying the bottle.

"You didn't hear?" Wade asked. "She and Jordan have been home for nearly two weeks."

"I only got back an hour before you called and I haven't talked to anyone else." Steve's voice was gruff. "Jordan's her husband?"

"Her son," Wade said gently. He wasn't blind; he'd noticed the resemblance. Lily and Steve had similar coloring, and the boy took after his mom, so it wasn't a clear bet plus she wasn't talking, at least not to Wade.

"Huh." Steve relaxed. "How about that," he added casually.

Wade was tempted to ask how the two of them had parted, but he didn't want to invite a discussion on his own situation, so he let it pass. "What do you think of the Mariners' chances this year?" he asked instead.

"Same as usual," Steve replied. "They'll have a decent season and choke in the play-offs."

After a few minutes of companionable silence, Steve got to his feet. "I think I'll throw a couple of steaks on the grill," he said. "Sound good?"

"Excellent. What can I do?" Wade asked.

"Enjoy the view and help with KP."

"Works for me," Wade drawled, turning back to the sight of numerous sailboats skimming across the water. Peaceful as the scene was, it didn't distract him from the events of the last two days.

He'd been over and over Pauline's accusations. He'd asked himself honestly if he'd been attracted to Lily or whether his behavior could have given that impression. Every time he pictured the fury on Pauline's face, he was filled with righteous anger all over again. She should have let him explain.

And yet, when he tried to convince himself that he'd dodged a bullet, escaped a crazy woman, gotten out in the nick of time, somehow he wasn't either reassured or relieved.

Right now he didn't know exactly what he was feeling, but it wasn't positive. It just felt all wrong.

When Pauline got home from the shop several days after Wade's departure, Dolly had returned from her cruise. She and Lily were sitting on the patio with a pitcher of lemonade.

"Come and join us," Dolly invited, holding up an empty glass. "I've got pictures of the trip and a present for you."

"Let me change into something looser first," Pauline

replied after she'd greeted her sister and given Dolly a hug. "I'll be right back."

Lily must have filled Dolly in about Wade, because she didn't mention him when Pauline joined them a few minutes later. Instead she described to both women the leisurely cruise of the Hawaiian Islands.

Pauline was content to enjoy the breeze and her lemonade while Dolly passed around the photos she and her lady friend had taken.

"This was our swimming instructor, Shawn," Dolly said with a sigh, holding up a picture of a teak-skinned hunk with his arm around her shoulders. She wore a one-piece bathing suit with a modest neckline and a little skirt. "If I could have gotten him in my bag, I might have brought him home with me," she added with a wink that made both sisters laugh.

"He'd be a better souvenir than one of those plastic hula dancers," Lily said drily.

"Oh, dear! Speaking of plastic hula dancers, I almost forgot your present." Dolly took a small box from the bag by her chair and handed it to Pauline.

Lily's cheeks turned pink. "Not that they aren't great," she said quickly. "I didn't mean—"

Dolly patted her hand. "I know, dear, and now I have a good idea what to bring you back the next time I go."

Pauline untied the ribbon and opened the box, which held a pair of simple black pearl earrings.

"Oh, Dolly, thank you. These are lovely." She showed them to Lily.

"They're okay," Lily deadpanned, "just not as neat as *my idea*."

"Next time, I promise." Dolly smiled at Lily. "I like your sister, Pauline."

Normally a comment like that would make her feel as though she'd been compared to Lily and found wanting, but today for some reason she was able to take it at face value. Besides, Dolly liked pretty much everyone she met.

"Is Jordan inside?" Pauline asked, glancing around the backyard.

"He was invited to a sleepover at the Branson boy's house. Remember Jeb from school? We met his family last week at a beach picnic."

Pauline nodded, remembering how excluded she'd felt at the time. Now that Wade had moved out, things like that didn't seem very important. "Did Jeb tell you he's a county sheriff now?" she asked.

"Oh, yeah." Lily grinned. "I figured Jordan needs exposure to guys like that."

"I think I'll fix a sandwich with some of that leftover ham I saw," Dolly said abruptly. "Anyone else?"

"No, thanks," Lily replied.

"Me neither," Pauline said. "I ate a late lunch."

After Dolly had gone inside, an awkward silence fell. Lily refilled Pauline's glass and then her own. "You've been very patient in not asking any questions about me," she said quietly. "Do you want to know what I've been doing all this time?"

Pauline was too curious to resist the offer. "Only what you want to tell me." Instead of looking at Lily, she studied the intense blue flowers on the hydrangea bush in the corner.

"I guess I should start at the beginning." Lily folded her hands in her lap. "A couple of months after I got to L.A., I met a dear man named Francis Yost at a cattle call, an open audition," she explained. "He invited me to lunch. I'd just found out that I was pregnant, so I was feeling desperate and I figured he might help me find a job."

"You could have come home," Pauline felt compelled to mention as she absorbed the confirmation of Jordan's parentage. "Steve would have stood by you and so would I."

Lily smiled sadly. "I don't suppose I was thinking too clearly at the time." Her eyes shimmered with unshed tears as she gazed down at her hands. "Francis offered me a place to stay. I was with him until his death three months ago."

"I'm sorry," Pauline murmured, but part of her sympathy was with Steve for never knowing about his son. "You should talk to Steve, you know."

Lily's eyes widened in alarm. "I will, but I'm just not ready."

It wasn't Pauline's place to interfere. "Did you want to marry Francis?" she asked curiously.

Lily shook her head. "I didn't love him in that way," she said vaguely. "We were happy, though, and Jordan adored him."

Pauline didn't know what to say.

For a moment, Lily seemed lost in memories. Then she sighed and set down her glass. "Anyway," she continued, turning to face Pauline, "I know it's a few years overdue, but I wanted to apologize again for what happened with Carter."

At first when Pauline had found Carter kissing Lily at her graduation party, Pauline had been too stunned to speak. When he'd noticed her, he'd started babbling some explanation that she didn't hear while Lily fled in tears.

With uncharacteristic impulsiveness, Pauline had yanked off his ring and thrown it at him. Only later that night, when she'd replayed the scene in her mind, had she realized that Lily had been struggling to get away from him.

Before Pauline had the chance to talk to Lily, she'd emptied her savings account and left for L.A. to "become a star." Since she was eighteen and left a note, there had been nothing Pauline could do. Of course, if she had known that Lily was pregnant, she would have insisted on helping.

"Did you ever think about coming home for a visit?" she asked Lily now.

Lily looked down at her hands. "I was ashamed that I hurt you after everything you did for me," she replied, her voice barely above a whisper.

After a moment, Pauline reached over and patted Lily's shoulder. Knowing she was sorry would help to put the whole ugly incident in the past where it belonged. The words seemed to lift the burden from her heart. "You actually did me a favor," she admitted. "I would never have been happy with Carter."

"On that I have to agree," Lily replied.

Impulsively Pauline stood up and opened her arms. With a sob, Lily scrambled to her feet.

"I missed you," she exclaimed. The two of them hugged each other, laughing and crying together.

Everything wasn't instantly perfect between them, Pauline realized. No doubt there would be more disagreements in the future, especially with Lily here in the house. But at least they had made a start. As she held her sister tight, she wished her broken relationship with Wade were as easy to mend.

"Pauline, telephone," Dolly called through the open kitchen window.

She hadn't even heard it ring. "I'll be right there." Surely Dolly would have mentioned if it was Wade, but Pauline didn't expect him to call, not after the way she had acted.

"Excuse me," she told Lily. "I'd better take it."

"Go ahead." Lily dabbed at her eyes. "And thanks."

"You, too," Pauline replied before hurrying up the stairs. At least meals around here would be less awkward now.

When she answered the phone, the children's librarian was on the other end of the line.

"Since I'm leaving on vacation before your next story hour," said Mrs. Coles, "I wondered if you could stop by the library for a few minutes tomorrow after work so we can discuss the books you're going to read."

"No problem," Pauline replied. "I should be able to get there by six-thirty, if that works for you."

"Perfect," Mrs. Coles agreed. "It's my late night to work, so I'll see you then."

As usual, Pauline drove home from the shop, then walked the few blocks to the library. Something must be going on in the large meeting room, because the parking lot was nearly full of cars.

Glad she hadn't driven, she went through the double front doors. By the time she saw Wade walking straight toward her, it was too late to detour or pretend she hadn't spotted him.

As they came face-to-face, she nearly forgot to breathe. "Hi," she said as her gaze roamed his face. "How have you been?"

He didn't smile as he looked back at her. "Fine, I guess. You?"

"Dolly's back from her cruise," Pauline babbled, wishing she could beg his forgiveness but too conscious of the flow of people all around them. Apparently the meeting had just broken up. "She had a great time."

"That's good." He glanced past Pauline as though he longed to escape.

She searched for the words to heal the icy breach between them, but her brain refused to cooperate. As he backed away, she noticed the stack of books under his arm. "Were you doing research on your sea captain?" she asked desperately.

He nodded as someone jostled him. "We're blocking traffic," he said. "Look, I need to get going. You take care."

Before she could even say goodbye, he walked past her toward the exit.

Refusing to turn and watch him walk out of her life once again, she hurried inside, letting the cool air bathe her burning cheeks. By sheer determination, she got through her meeting with the librarian without breaking down. The moment they were finished, Pauline wished her a happy vacation and fled.

She practically ran all the way home. When she walked into the kitchen, Lily was sitting at the table sipping a glass of white wine as she flipped through a magazine.

"Where is everyone?" Pauline asked.

"Dolly was tired, so she's gone to bed early. My son, the social butterfly freshly emerged from his cocoon, is staying at the Bransons' for another night."

Her eyes narrowed as she studied Pauline in the same way she had when they were younger. "What's wrong? To enlist an overused cliché, you look like you've just seen a ghost."

Lily's question was all it took to open the floodgates on Pauline's misery. With her vision blurred by the tears she'd been struggling to hold back, she collapsed into the chair opposite her sister and covered her face in her hands.

"Are you hurt?" Lily fetched her a tissue from the box on the counter. "Tell me what happened."

"I saw Wade at the library," Pauline blubbered. Embarrassed by her lack of control, she blotted her eyes while Lily poured a second glass of wine. "He looked so normal, certainly not like a man who's suffering."

"The bastard," Lily said mildly. "Here, drink this." She gave the wine to Pauline and then sat back down. "I'll bet that underneath all that male bravado, he's just as torn up as you are. Men hide their feelings better, but they get ulcers and high blood pressure."

Pauline blew her nose and took a big gulp of wine.

She couldn't help but remember how she and Lily used to sit cross-legged on one of their beds, discussing everything. It would be incredibly easy to fall back into the habit of confiding in her as though the last thirteen years had never happened.

"Did you talk to him?" Lily persisted.

"Some meeting let out and there were people everywhere." Fresh tears spilled down Pauline's cheeks. "I miss him so much," she whispered hoarsely, giving in to the need to talk.

"You should call him," Lily said decisively. "Tell him that you want to see him." She took a sip of her wine. "Heck, tell him he left something important behind when he moved and you have to give it to him."

Pauline shook her head before her sister was even done speaking. "Lily, I raised my hand to him. I've never hit anyone since you cut off my Barbie's hair and I socked you in the arm. But I nearly slapped him."

Lily's lips twitched. "I remember that doll. I told Mom and she made you sit in the corner."

"Tattletale," Pauline said with a watery grin.

"Brat," Lily replied, smiling. Instantly her expression sobered. "You're in love with Wade, aren't you?"

Pauline nodded glumly. "'Fraid so."

"What do you have to lose if he refuses to listen?" Lily asked.

Lily had probably never had a man refuse to listen to her in her life, Pauline thought wryly. She didn't understand rejection or humiliation as well as Pauline did. After the story had made the rounds about Carter and Lily, Pauline had gotten to know humiliation intimately—especially when several other men, one of them married, offered with winks and leers to "console" her.

"I'll think about what you said," she agreed just to keep the peace. "Thanks."

Lily reached across the table to squeeze her hand. "I thought I'd take Jordan to the cemetery one day," she said. "You know, to show him where his grandma and grandpa are."

"That's a nice idea," Pauline agreed, relieved by the change of subject. There were worse things than breaking up, and dying too young was certainly one of them.

"I was jealous of you, you know," Lily added. "You and Dad were so close."

Pauline's jaw dropped at the admission. "Are you serious? Our parents *doted* on you, Mom always dressing you up and fixing your hair, Dad showing you off. What did you, the little princess, have to be jealous of?" She couldn't keep the disbelief from her voice. Was this Lily's awkward way of trying to make her feel better? If so, it was too ridiculous to work.

"Sure, they treated me like a doll they could show off," Lily agreed. "But Dad listened to you. He knew you had a brain." She twirled the stem of her glass between her fingers. "He thought I was cute, but he never expected me to *think*. Mom would be braiding my hair, talking about fashion or some other fluff. Then you'd walk in and she'd tell you about something she'd heard on the news or ask your opinion. It used to drive me bonkers."

Her tone and the way she rolled her eyes seemed

sincere, but Pauline wasn't convinced. "They couldn't have thought I was too smart," she protested. "They were always on me about my grades, especially in high school."

"Because they knew you could get A's," Lily insisted. "They didn't expect me to do well or to go to college like you, so they were perfectly happy with my C's and B's. They never required more of me, so neither did I." Her smile was edged with sadness. "Then Francis offered to send me back to school so that I could learn accounting and manage his books. I realized that I'm smart, too."

"Well, I'll be darned." Pauline sat back in her chair and stared at her sister. "Sounds as though we both wanted things we weren't getting."

"Your brain and my looks," Lily agreed. "Never realizing that each of us has both."

Chapter Fourteen

On Saturday the sunny weather and the height of the tourist season brought a steady flow of customers to Uncommon Threads. Pauline was grateful for Bertie's help at the shop, especially since her own inability to sleep through the night and her lack of appetite were taking their toll on her energy level. If time was the great healer, as people claimed, it was clear that mending a broken heart would take longer than a couple of weeks.

Funny, but she didn't remember hurting like this after her breakup with Carter. What she had felt then was anger and embarrassment, not pain and regret.

When the bell over the front door of the shop jangled for the umpteenth time, she glanced up from the order she was bagging, pleasantly surprised to see Lily.

"I'll be with you in a minute," Pauline told her. Although the two of them certainly still experienced awkward moments, Pauline was encouraged by their growing closeness. Lily's beauty and outgoing personality didn't bug Pauline as much as they always had either, especially since Lily's startling confession that she, too, had been jealous.

Go figure.

"I was hoping you'd come in to see the shop again," Pauline said, joining Lily as she wandered around.

"You've really made some changes," Lily replied, examining one of the revolving display racks. "I remember what a little hole-in-the-wall it used to be, but now it's charming. You must be proud."

"Thanks," Pauline murmured. "It's nice of you to say so." She introduced Lily to Bertie, who stood shyly behind the counter. It was obvious to Pauline that she was intimidated.

"What a lovely necklace," Lily exclaimed when she saw the beaded strands that Bertie wore. "Did you make it yourself?"

As Lily leaned closer, Bertie's blush deepened. Her smile, though, grew. "I even made the beads." Shyness forgotten, she talked to Lily for several minutes while Pauline rang up another sale. When she was done, Lily came over to the counter.

"Actually, I have some news," she told Pauline. "I ran into a friend from school, Bonnie Denny, and she told me about a house that another friend of hers wants to sublet for a year while he works in Japan."

"Oh?" Pauline braced herself, feelings mixed.

Lily twirled a strand of her hair. "It's perfect for Jordan and me, Paulie. I want to get settled into a place of our own before school starts, so we'll be moving at the first of the month."

"I understand," Pauline replied, hiding the rush of disappointment. Perhaps after they left she'd try again to find another boarder. "Dolly and I will miss you both."

"The other reason I came by," Lily added, "is to invite you on a picnic after work."

"Oh, thanks, but I don't think so." All Pauline wanted to do was go home and rest.

"No, I insist," Lily said with surprising stubbornness. "I want the two of us to spend some time at that little beach where we used to go when we were teenagers. Remember? It's the one with the great tide pools."

How could Pauline forget? The last time she had been there was with Wade. After they'd eaten and walked along the water, they had made love in a sheltered area, giggling and whispering about being discovered.

"I don't want to," she said stubbornly.

"Just do this one thing for me," Lily pleaded. "We've come so far, and I want us to revisit our special place before Jordan and I move out." Like a bloodhound, she must have been able to scent Pauline's weakening. "You don't have to do a thing except show up," Lily promised. "I'll get sandwiches and salad from that great deli down by the waterfront park. All you need to do is to meet me at the beach."

"Why don't we ride together?" Pauline regretted not

sticking by her guns, but she couldn't back out now and disappoint Lily, who looked as excited as a kid with a new balloon.

"I have to pick Jordan up at the park and then drop him off at another boy's house to play," Lily said. "It's just easier for me to pick up the food and meet you there after work. What's a good time?"

Pauline thought for a minute. "Seven-thirty? Is that too late?"

"No, that's perfect," Lily said. "I'll see you then, so don't let me down."

By the time Pauline locked up the shop for the night, that was *exactly* what she was tempted to do. A group of women from a Canadian tour bus had come in right before closing, determined to spend the rest of their American money before going home.

Pauline was running more than a half hour late, but sales for the day had been good. At this rate, she might have enough money saved for her dream. When Mr. Grimes next door retired, she wanted to lease his space. It would give her the room she needed to carry yarn and other knitting supplies.

There wasn't time for her to go home before meeting Lily, but her loose-fitting cotton pants and flowered camp shirt were comfortable, and her canvas shoes would be fine for walking on the rocky beach.

When she arrived at the parking spot, Lily's empty car was already there above the thicket of trees and shrubs that hid the beach from the road. The path wasn't steep, and the view from the outcropping of rocks above the sheltered strip of sand and pebbles was beautiful. Sometimes Pauline sat on a flat rock and watched the barges and container ships heading for the ports in Seattle and Tacoma. Once, she had seen an aircraft carrier on its way to the naval base in Everett.

Today she barely glanced at Admiralty Inlet or the hazy shoreline of Whidbey Island as she made her way down the familiar path. The sun was near to sinking behind the Olympic Mountains behind her, so the uneven ground was shaded, but she had no trouble.

Inhaling the welcome scents of salt and seaweed, she rounded the last granite boulder. Massive driftwood logs, hurled onto the beach during some long-ago storm, lay half-buried above the tide mark. Beyond them, the cove appeared empty except for an unfamiliar blanket and a small cooler.

Lily must have decided to explore some of the tide pools that were hidden from view while she waited. When they were children, the two of them had spent many hours watching the hermit crabs, minnows and other tiny creatures trapped in the shallow depressions worn into the rocks by the receding water.

Content to watch the waves, Pauline settled onto the blanket with her back resting against a log and waited. She could feel the tension drain away as she opened the cooler in search of something cold to drink.

To her surprise, there was a folded piece of paper on top of the food. Warily she opened it and immediately recognized Lily's handwriting.

I hope this balances the scales, was written in flowing script.

Pauline had no idea what the words meant, but as she folded the paper back up and looked around, it wasn't her sister who emerged from behind a large boulder.

Wearing a serious expression, it was Wade who picked his way over the rocks.

Pauline bolted to her feet, tucking a loose strand of hair behind her ear.

"What are you doing here?" she choked as the muscles locked in her throat. "Where's Lily?"

Was this some cruel joke the two of them had cooked up? As soon as the thought formed, Pauline dismissed it. Neither of them was the kind of person who would hurt anyone deliberately.

Removing his sunglasses, Wade closed the distance between them as Pauline's heart began banging against the wall of her chest. Although she'd just seen him, he appeared even more attractive than she remembered. He'd gotten his hair cut short again and he was freshly shaved.

"Lily's not coming," he said, stopping a few feet away with his hands jammed into the pockets of his khaki shorts. "I see that you found her note."

Pauline waved the paper in the air. She could have screamed in frustration. "But what does it have to do with you?"

He shrugged, a muscle jumping in his cheek. "Depends on what you want."

She bit her lip, wishing she'd had the time to prepare what to say. "I'm sorry," she blurted, shaking her head. "Please believe me when I say that I never meant to hurt you."

To her surprise, he squeezed his eyes shut as he averted his face. "So she was wrong after all," he muttered.

If anything, Pauline was more confused than ever. "Wrong about what? That I regret all those terrible things I said to you? That I should have trusted you and had more faith in you?" She swallowed. "It's no excuse, I know, but loving you made me crazy. It scared me half to death."

His head whipped back around and he stared, his eyes suddenly as dark as an ocean storm. "What did you say?" he demanded.

"I love you," she said simply, letting the note fall from her fingers as she dropped her hands to her sides.

"Just not enough to trust me."

For the first time, she recognized her ability to cause him pain, even though she was afraid to wonder why. "Could we sit down?" She gestured toward the big log.

They settled onto the blanket with a couple of feet separating them so they could face each other.

"I've always been envious of Lily," she admitted. "It blinded me to certain things."

"Why would you envy her?" Wade appeared to be genuinely puzzled. "She's pretty enough, if you like that type. But you've got the whole package—beauty, brains and sensuality oozing out of every pore."

Pauline could hardly believe her ears. *If you like the type?* She struggled to not break into hysterical giggles. Instead she repeated some of her conversation with Lily and what they had figured out between them.

"When I saw my fiancé trying to kiss her, my feelings of inferiority were confirmed," she concluded.

Wade reached over and squeezed her hand. "You must have loved him a lot. Now it's my turn to be jealous."

Wade's touch felt so good that she almost forgot what they were discussing. "Don't waste your time," she replied. "The reality was that I felt lonely and overwhelmed after our parents were killed. I was trying to create a new family with him."

Wade nodded with fresh understanding in his eyes. "Sharon's affair devastated me, too, so I guess it's normal to doubt yourself when someone you count on lets you down. She tried to justify her affair with John by accusing me of cheating on her first. I realized that she didn't know me at all."

"Are you going to stay here in Crescent Cove?" Pauline asked meekly.

"I'm thinking about opening my own consulting office," he said firmly. "I was good at helping people grow their money, so that's what I plan to do."

Pauline had a sudden brainstorm. "Lily's going to start her own business, too, as a CPA. If you shared an office, you could both save on staffing and equipment."

Wade studied her face silently.

"It was probably a dumb idea," she said hastily. "Forget I said anything."

"You wouldn't mind if Lily and I did that?" he asked.

"I kind of like the idea. Will you consider it?"

"Only if you consider a suggestion of mine in return," he said hesitantly.

The tightness she'd felt in her chest since she'd first

seen him began to loosen. He wasn't leaving town and they were talking. It was a start.

"If you're going to ask whether I've rented your apartment or your old set of rooms, I haven't," she volunteered. "You can move back if you want to."

Wade shook his head. "Sorry, but I've set my sights a little higher than that."

Her hopes plummeted and her cheeks grew hot. Of course he would want something fancier than her old house. He'd probably found a place on the water. "I understand."

"No more running back and forth between my bed and yours," he added softly.

While she attempted to process his comment, he slid to one knee in the sand.

Her breath stopped in her chest. "What are you doing?" she blurted.

"Proposing," he drawled. "Let me say my piece, okay?"

Speech wasn't an option for her at the moment. All she could do was bob her head.

Wade enfolded her chilled hands in both of his. "I came to Crescent Cove looking for a new start. Love wasn't part of my plan." His expression was so tender that she had to blink quickly to keep from crying. "Then I met you." His voice grew husky. "Honey, I'm yours if you'll have me. What do you say?"

Pauline let out a shriek that must have frightened the seagulls. "Yes, absolutely yes!" she exclaimed, throwing her arms around him so that he lost his balance and they fell over sideways onto the blanket.

Wade shifted to face her. "I love you," he whispered. Then he kissed her with all the passion and love that she had ever dreamed about.

When they finally let each other go, he helped her sit up. "Are you hungry?" he asked with a crooked grin.

"Famished!" Suddenly a lightbulb went off in her brain. "I get it," she exclaimed. "I get Lily's note about balancing the scales. Oh, my God! I've got to call her and share our news."

"Then can I eat?" he asked.

Suddenly the pieces all fell into place. "Were you in cahoots with her or did she coerce you, too?" Pauline demanded, suddenly suspicious—but not in a bad way.

"She left me a message on Steve's machine to call her," he replied. "I thought he was going to pass out when he heard her voice."

Interesting, Pauline mused as she hit her home number. "Oh, man!" she exclaimed after several failed attempts. "I can't get through, so we'll have to leave right away."

"Uh-uh." Wade opened the cooler, pulling out a split of champagne and two glasses that were hidden beneath a towel. "First we're going to celebrate."

"Did you bring root beer in case I said no?" she asked curiously.

As he opened the champagne, he shook his head. "Failure wasn't an option," he said. "You can trust me on that."

* * * * *

Page-turning drama...

Exotic, glamorous locations...

Intense emotion and passionate seduction...

Sheikhs, princes and billionaire tycoons...

This summer, may we suggest:

THE SHEIKH'S DISOBEDIENT BRIDE
by Jane Porter

On sale June.

AT THE GREEK TYCOON'S BIDDING
by Cathy Williams

On sale July.

THE ITALIAN MILLIONAIRE'S VIRGIN WIFE

On sale August.

With new titles to choose from every month,
discover a world of romance in our books written
by internationally bestselling authors.

HARLEQUIN® *Presents*

It's the ultimate in quality romance!

Available wherever Harlequin books are sold.

www.eHarlequin.com　　　HPGEN06

**Hidden in the secrets of antiquity,
lies the unimagined truth...**

Introducing

ROGUE
ANGEL™

a brand-new line filled with mystery
and suspense, action and adventure,
and a fascinating look into history.

And it all begins with DESTINY.

In a sealed crypt in
France, where the
terrifying legend of
the beast of Gevaudan
begins to unravel,
Annja Creed discovers
a stunning artifact
that will seal her destiny.

*Available every other
month starting
July 2006, wherever
you buy books.*

Hidden in the secrets
of antiquity, lies the
unimagined truth...

ROGUE
ANGEL
Alex
Archer
DESTINY

GOLD EAGLE 62119
$6.50 U.S./$7.99 CAN.

GRA1

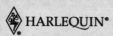

HARLEQUIN®

American ROMANCE®

IS PROUD TO PRESENT A GUEST APPEARANCE BY

QUILL
BOOK
AWARD
WINNING
AUTHOR

NEW YORK TIMES bestselling author

DEBBIE MACOMBER

The Wyoming Kid

The story of an ex–rodeo cowboy,
a schoolteacher and their journey to the altar.

"Best-selling Macomber, with more than
100 romances and women's fiction titles
to her credit, sure has a way of pleasing readers."
—*Booklist* on *Between Friends*

The Wyoming Kid is available from
Harlequin American Romance in July 2006.

Stability is highly overrated....

Dana Logan's world had always revolved around her children. Now they're all grown up and don't seem to need anything she's able to give them. Struggling to find her new identity, Dana realizes that it's about time for her to get "off her rocker" and begin a new life!

Off Her Rocker

by Jennifer Archer

HARLEQUIN®
Next™

#1771 BACK IN THE BACHELOR'S ARMS—Victoria Pade
Northbridge Nuptials
Years ago, when Chloe Carmichael was pregnant by high school
sweetheart Reid Walker, her meddling parents sent her out of town and
told Reid she'd lost the baby. Now Chloe was back to sell her parents'
old house—and *Dr.* Reid Walker was the buyer. Soon he discovered the
child he never knew…and rediscovered the woman he'd never forgotten.

#1772 FINDING NICK—Janis Reams Hudson
Tribute, Texas
Shannon Malloy's book about 9/11 heroes was almost done—but when
she tracked her last interview subject, injured New York firefighter
Nick Carlucci, to Tribute, Texas, he wasn't talking. While Nick denied
Shannon access to his story, he couldn't deny her access to his heart—
especially when he realized their shared connection to the tragedy….

#1773 THE PERFECT WIFE—Judy Duarte
Talk of the Neighborhood
Rich, thin Carly Anderson had a fairy-tale life…until her husband left
her for her friend down the street. Carly became reclusive—maybe even
chubby!—but when worried neighbors coaxed her out to the local pool,
she was pleasantly surprised to meet carpenter Bo Conway. Would this
down-to-earth man help Carly get to *happily ever after* after all?

#1774 OUTBACK BABY—Lilian Darcy
Wanted: Outback Wives
City girl Shay Russell had come to the Australian Outback in flood
season to rethink her values. And when she dropped into cattleman Dusty
Tanner's well-ordered life after a helicopter crash, two worlds literally
collided. Soon, not only the waters, but the passions, were running high
on the Outback….until Shay told Dusty she was pregnant.

#1775 THE PRODIGAL M.D. RETURNS—Marie Ferrarella
The Alaskans
Things really heated up in Hades, Alaska, when skirt-chasing
Ben Kerrigan came back to town. But after leaving Heather Ryan
Kendall at the altar seven years ago, Dr. Ben was a reformed man.
Soon Ben was back paying Heather personal house calls…but recently
widowed Heather and her six-year-old daughter had a surprise for the
prodigal M.D.

#1776 JESSIE'S CHILD—Lois Faye Dyer
The McClouds of Montana
Even a decades-old family feud couldn't stop Jessie McCloud and Zack
Kerrigan from sharing a night of passion—just one night. But four years
later, when Zack returned from military duty overseas, he discovered
that *just one night* had had lifelong consequences. Could Jessie and
Zack overcome dueling family traditions to raise their son…together?